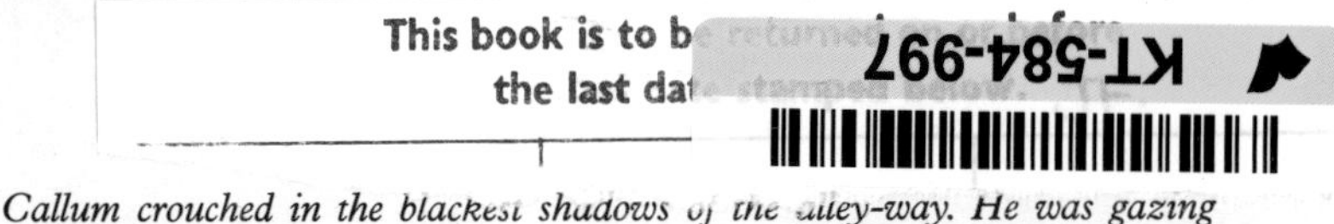

Callum crouched in the blackest shadows of the alley-way. He was gazing intently at the front door of the house across the street. It was crazy to hang around here. But he just couldn't help staying to watch.

When Callum set fire to his own home to take revenge on his mother's boyfriend, Nick, he had no idea of the disastrous chain of events he was to set in motion. Who was the weird android-like figure crouching by the incubator at the chemical company where his dad works? Why was his dad having secret meetings with Nick? And what was happening to the trees in the forest? Throughout all these strange events, the squirrel seems to be the only thing Callum can rely on.

Susan Gates was born in Grimsby in 1950. She has a degree in English and American Literature from Warwick University and a Dip. Ed. from Coventry College of Education. She has taught in secondary schools in Africa and for eight years in a comprehensive school in County Durham. She has also taught in a technical college and on YTS and Community Task Force Schemes. She is married and has three children.

Also by Susan Gates

Deadline for Danny's Beach

ISBN 0 19 271696 4

'. . . a fast-moving and thoughtful tale about something many readers will have experienced—the contamination of local beaches.'

Times Educational Supplement

African Dreams

ISBN 0 19 271684 0

'Susan Gates has an impressive understanding of the feelings which drive young people . . . reading *African Dreams* will be a valuable social education as well as a pleasure.'

The School Librarian

Raider

ISBN 0 19 271644 1

'. . . it is still possible to find new fiction that can be read even next year, or later, or twice by the same reader. *Raider* is one for a start.'

The Observer

FIREBUG

OTHER BOOKS BY SUSAN GATES

The Burnhope Wheel
The Lock
Dragline
Deadline for Danny's Beach
African Dreams
Raider

FIREBUG

SUSAN GATES

Oxford University Press
Oxford New York Toronto

Oxford University Press, Walton Street, Oxford OX2 6DP

Oxford New York
Athens Auckland Bangkok Bombay
Calcutta Cape Town Dar es Salaam Delhi
Florence Hong Kong Istanbul Karachi
Kuala Lumpur Madras Madrid Melbourne
Mexico City Nairobi Paris Singapore
Taipei Tokyo Toronto

and associated companies in
Berlin Ibadan

Oxford is a trade mark of Oxford University Press

First published 1996

A CIP catalogue record for this book is available from the British Library

ISBN 0 19 271735 9

Cover design by Slatter–Anderson
Cover illustration from Images Colour Library

Printed and bound in Great Britain by
Biddles Ltd, Guildford and King's Lynn

1

Callum crouched in the blackest shadows of the alley-way. He was gazing intently at the front door of the house across the street. It was crazy to hang around here. He should have been running now, putting as much distance between himself and this place as possible. But he just couldn't help staying to watch.

He had his jacket hood up so no one would recognize him. The drawstring was pulled tight, leaving only a small hole. All you could see was a cold white nose and two glittering eyes.

Nervously, Callum rattled the box of matches in his pocket.

Nothing was going to happen.

Yes, it was.

Behind the glass panels in the front door of the house there was a weird orange glow. It throbbed, like the windows of an alien spacecraft. The paint on the door was blistering. The blisters swelled, then popped like bubble gum.

Callum held his breath. In his eyes, which were almost all you could see of his face, was a strange expression. It was a mixture of terror, excitement—and pride.

Through the glass, Callum could see small flames now. They were racing upwards like squirrels up a tree. That was the blue curtain burning. The one that you pulled over the front door to keep the draughts out. Callum knew about the curtain because his mother had made it last winter. He had just set fire to his own house.

Callum forgot about running away. As black smoke leaked through the letterbox he watched, fascinated. The street was absolutely quiet. The fire was still his secret. It made him grin to think of everyone watching telly, deaf and blind to the real drama happening right on their doorsteps.

He felt surprisingly calm. He felt in control, even powerful. As if those savage flames were doing his bidding. As if they were expressing all his pain and hatred for him. And in a deadlier, more spectacular way than he ever could.

'Just try. Just try to ignore that, Dr Nick Sharp,' muttered Callum through the spy-hole in his coat.

Then the wail of a fire engine smashed the silence, threw him into panic.

'Too soon,' he gabbled to himself. 'Way too soon.'

He would have phoned them himself. From the phone box on the corner. When he was good and ready.

But he'd lost control. It wasn't his fire any more.

His whole body jumped with alarm when the fire engine swung into his street. It came screaming down towards him, blue lights whirling.

And, suddenly, everything was chaos. Callum's private show had become a public one. He had to give up his ringside seat. He shrank right back into the dark heart of the alley. There were people yelling, rushing everywhere, lights flashing, firemen trampling the garden flowers.

Callum pulled his hood even tighter. He looked like a wide-eyed, frightened seal pup peering out through an ice hole.

'We've got him!'

'He's OK. We don't need the stretcher.'

'Move out the way there!'

'Give him a whiff of oxygen.'

* * *

Callum should have stayed hidden. But he had to see what he had done. He couldn't help himself.

He moved out of the cover of the alley. There was a big audience now. People in slippers, some in dressing gowns, standing silently watching.

Callum hid behind them. He didn't want any of the neighbours to recognize him. He could just see, through a gap between two women. One of them was Mrs Petronelli. She was big. She was wearing a pink fluffy bathrobe.

The front door of his house was open. Inside was a smoke-blackened cave. But the fire hadn't done much damage. The firemen had stopped it too soon. The stairs looked OK. And he could see through to the kitchen. That was untouched.

Callum sighed. But he wasn't sure whether it was relief, or disappointment.

Then his gaze shifted. And he saw him—Nick, Mum's boyfriend. He was sitting on the front garden wall. He had a blanket slung round his shoulders. And he was breathing through a mask which he held over his mouth and nose. There were firemen around him, rolling up hoses, talking into radio receivers. But none of them seemed to be paying him much attention.

Then he lifted his head, took off the mask and looked straight at Callum. At first Callum didn't believe it, still thought he hadn't been spotted. But then, with a sick gulp of horror, he realized that Mrs Petronelli had got bored and gone home to watch TV and that there was no one to hide him. Callum felt as exposed as if a searchlight had picked him out. And someone had said, like in a film, 'Freeze! Or we shoot!'

So he stood there, frozen to the spot, his eyes locked with Nick's eyes. Nick's eyes were ice-blue behind round, gold rimmed specs.

An ambulance swerved round the corner. Neither of them noticed it.

Nick lifted his right hand. He made his first two fingers into the barrel of a gun and his thumb and his other two fingers into the trigger. He sighted along his fingers straight at Callum. And Callum saw his mouth shape the word, 'Bang!'

And Callum knew, without any shadow of doubt, that Nick knew that he had caused the fire.

He's got no proof, thought Callum wildly. He can't prove it!

Then a woman paramedic came up to Nick. She said something. He protested. Callum watched him turn his charming smile on her the way he did on Mum. But the paramedic didn't give in the way Mum always did. She wasn't so soft. She insisted. Nick shrugged. And allowed himself to be led away. Nick was tall and slim with a neat blond beard. As he walked towards the ambulance he took off his specs, flipped them closed and put them in the pocket of his shirt.

After he'd made the gun sign at Callum, Nick didn't once glance in his direction. He ignored him, as if Callum didn't exist.

And nobody else noticed Callum either. The fire engine sped off to another emergency. The ambulance pulled away. The onlookers hung around for a while, as if waiting for something else to happen. Then they too drifted away. The show was over.

Callum stood on his own, under the cold white glare of a street lamp.

A police car nosed round the corner.

And suddenly Callum was off like a hare. He raced down the alley, across a street. A driver blasted his horn as Callum bodyswerved the bonnet of his car.

But Callum didn't stop until, panting, with burning lungs, he arrived at a phone box.

He yanked the door open and collapsed inside. He dug into his pocket, scrabbled under the box of matches for the 10p piece he knew was there.

With trembling hands he put his money in the slot and punched in the number.

It rang. Nobody answered.

'Please be in,' sobbed Callum into the phone. 'Please be in.' His knuckles, grasping the mouthpiece, were white as bone.

The phone carried on ringing. Then someone picked it up.

'Dad! Is that you, Dad?' gasped Callum into the phone.

'Who's that? This is 75032. Have you got the wrong number?'

Callum took a deep breath, fought to keep his voice steady.

'Dad, it's me, Cal. I'm in terrible trouble, Dad. You have to come and get me.'

'Cal! What are you playing at, ringing this time of night? What are you talking about? What kind of trouble? Where's your mum? Let me talk to her.'

'She's not here, Dad. I'm ringing from a phone box. The one outside the Fortune Cookie take-away. Just hurry up, Dad,' begged Callum in an anguished, desperate voice. 'I'll wait here for you. Just come and get me. Please.'

2

Callum sat huddled on the back seat of Dad's car. He still had his hood up. He was shivering—it seemed ages before Dad had arrived to rescue him.

Callum's dad was a slight, wiry little man. He was quick-moving, active. He reminded you of an energetic gnome. At 36 he was already going bald. He wasn't an elegant dresser like Nick. He wore, as always, his shabby jeans, T-shirt, and trainers. Usually, he was fairly placid, easy-going. But tonight he was so mad that he could barely concentrate on his driving.

'I can't believe this stuff you're telling me!' His eyes blazed at Callum through the driving mirror. It startled Callum to see how shocked they were. 'Do you realize what you've done? I mean, have you done it before? Set fire to things?'

'No,' lied Callum. ''Course I haven't.'

'But you could've hurt Nick. You could've killed him. You didn't really want to hurt him, did you?'

'No,' lied Callum. ''Course not. I was just messing about.'

'Messing about?' yelled his dad, furiously. 'It was incredibly dangerous. Have you got any idea what a serious crime arson is? You could be put away for years! Does anyone know you did it?'

'No,' said Callum, uneasily. He couldn't help remembering Nick mouthing 'Bang!' at him.

'Well, that's a relief anyway,' sighed Callum's dad. Then he said, in his threatening voice, 'But I hope at least you're sorry—now you know how stupid you've been.'

'I am,' muttered Callum from deep inside his coat. He was sorry that he'd upset his dad. But he wasn't sorry about Nick.

'What did you say?' said Dad, half-twisting his head round.

'I am,' repeated Callum. 'I am sorry.' He knew it was what his dad wanted to hear. He would say anything, so long as Dad stopped talking to him as if he were a criminal.

'That still doesn't make it all right!' warned Dad. 'Not by a long way.'

But Callum could hear that his voice had softened.

Dad pulled up with a screech of brakes at a red light. He'd almost driven right through it. He turned round and glared at Callum. His eyes were still mad. But they were also hurt and bewildered.

'I can't believe you'd do something like that. What if Mum had been in the house?'

'She wasn't. She was out, at that singing group she goes to. And they all go on to the pub afterwards. I wouldn't hurt Mum!' protested Callum. 'And anyway, it was an accident.'

'Well, it was a bloody dangerous accident. And moronic. Promise me you'll never, ever do anything like that again.'

Before Callum could reply, the car behind them blasted its horn. The lights were green. Dad accelerated away.

'Promise me!' insisted Callum's dad.

'Well, I hate him,' exploded Callum from the back seat. 'He hates me as well. He says he'll throw me out when I'm sixteen. But Mum doesn't know what he's like. He's always greasing around her, with this soppy little-boy smile. It makes you sick! And she thinks he's so wonderful. Thinks the sun shines out his backside. I can't understand it—anyone can see what he's really like. He's horrible and sneaky. Always getting me into trouble, setting traps for me.

And I get blamed for everything and he turns Mum against me and he's such a smart-arse, such a smooth operator, so good with words that I get all mixed-up and I can't think of nothing to say 'cos he's so good at arguing and he's always got an answer and—'

Callum had to pause to gulp in some air.

'Does he hurt you?' interrupted Dad, his voice suddenly urgent. 'He doesn't hit you, does he?'

'No,' admitted Callum, slowly.

'That's all right then,' said Dad.

'It's not all right,' yelled Callum in desperate frustration. 'You don't understand what he's like. He—'

But before Callum could go on Dad said, almost wearily, 'Look, we'd better stop and phone Mum. She'll be worried sick. She'll wonder where you are. I should have thought of it before.'

But Callum was still all fired up. 'Why don't you just beat him up, Dad? Get tough? Wipe that greasy smile off his face. Why don't you come back, Dad? So it was like it was before?'

'It was terrible before,' muttered Callum's dad, in the same weary voice. 'Remember all those rows?'

'I just remember that no one told me anything,' said Callum in a bitter rush of words. 'I didn't know what was going on. And when I asked Mum if everything was OK she always said, "'Course it is!" And you said, "'Course it is!" And then I just came home one day after school and you'd moved out and Nick had moved in. Nobody told me anything!'

Dad bit his lip. 'Sorry, Cal,' he said. Then he said, 'But it can never be like it was before. I mean, before the rows. For a start, your mum doesn't want me to come back.'

'She'll change her mind,' said Callum, eagerly. 'Go on, Dad, give Nick a good kicking!'

Callum's dad sighed, shook his head. 'Look,' he said, 'here's a phone box. Call Mum. She'll be home by now. She'll be worrying. Your summer holidays started on Friday, didn't they? You could stay with me for a few days. Long as your mum says it's OK.'

Callum didn't want to call his mum just yet. He liked the idea of her worrying about him. But he didn't dare say this to Dad. For a meek little bloke Dad had looked quite fierce just now when he was in a rage. I bet he could give Nick a hammering, thought Callum, wistfully.

'Go on, phone her. Here's some change.'

Callum trudged to the phone, shut himself in, punched in the numbers.

At the other end the phone was snatched up immediately.

'It's me, Mum.'

'Cal! I've been worried sick! Where are you?'

'It's all right, Mum, I'm with Dad. I met him in town—he took me for a McDonald's and we—'

'Have you got any idea what's been going on back here?'

Callum made his eyes all wide and innocent, even though his mum couldn't see him. 'No,' he said.

It took three ten-pence-worths of time for his mum to tell Callum what he already knew.

'And Nick is OK,' she said. 'That's the main thing.'

Callum made a hideous monster-face at the other end of the phone.

'I've just come from the hospital,' she said. 'They've only got him in for observation. He was really lucky. He could have burnt the place down.'

'What?' said Callum.

'He did it himself, the silly man. He told the police all about it. He left a cigarette in the ashtray in the hall. You know, the one next to the phone. And, somehow, it set fire to the curtain.'

Callum's face scrunched into a frown. Simultaneously he thought: I'm off the hook! and Why did Nick say he did it? It didn't make any sense . . .

'So are you coming straight home?' Mum was saying.

'I might stay with Dad for a bit,' said Callum. He said it casually. But he meant it to be a threat.

But, to his dismay, Mum did not protest. She said, 'What a good idea.' She sounded suspiciously relieved.

Callum immediately lost his temper. Beep, beep, beep, went the phone. He rammed in his last 10p and started shouting before the line cleared. 'He's always getting at me, Mum. He doesn't like me. He—'

Callum's mum broke in, trying to calm him down. 'Look, Cal, don't get so worked up. He's a sweet man, honestly. Really sweet. I don't know why you don't like him. You don't give him a chance. I mean, he's been really patient with you, really good in the circumstances and—'

'I'm staying with Dad!' yelled Callum into the phone. Up until that moment he'd been undecided. But now he was sure. 'I might stay with him for the whole summer.'

'Look,' said Mum, 'I can't talk to you when you're in this mood. When you get back to Dad's get him to call me and we'll—'

Callum had already slammed the phone down on her.

He stomped back to the car, yanked the door open, crashed it shut behind him.

'Mind that door! What did she say?' asked Dad.

'Says it's OK,' muttered Callum. 'She didn't like it though—she wants me at home really. She says for you to phone her when we get back.'

Callum's dad nodded and started up the car.

'Is Nick OK?' he asked Callum.

'Huh!' snorted Callum from the back seat. ''Course he's OK.'

'Did the fire cause much damage?'

'No,' said Callum. 'It got put out. But the funny thing, Dad, is that Nick says he did it. Says he left a cigarette burning. What did he say that for?'

'Maybe he was covering for you,' said Dad. 'I thought you said nobody knew.'

'He wouldn't cover for me,' muttered Callum. 'He'd get me put away if he could.'

'What did you say?'

'Nothing.'

'Well,' said Dad, 'maybe he did leave a cigarette burning. Maybe he really thought it was him. It's a piece of good luck for you. Because it means the police won't be looking for anyone else.'

'I told you it was an accident!' protested Callum, automatically.

But he felt dizzy with relief. The idea of his good luck amazed him. He'd had nothing but bad luck, lately.

Dad's right, he was thinking. Nick can't know it's me. He must really think he did it. That must be it, he decided.

That must be it because, otherwise, Nick would have grabbed the chance to blame him for the fire. They would have locked me away, thought Callum, remembering what his dad had said. And Nick would've just loved that. To get me out the way, so he's got Mum all to himself. Well, he's missed his chance, hasn't he? Ha, ha, ha!

But he still felt uneasy. That Nick was slippery as a barrel of eels.

They had left town now and the motorway. It was pitch black with only the lights of scattered farms shining out over dark fields. Like lone ships in the ocean. Callum stared gloomily out of the car windows. He didn't like the country. There was nothing to do there.

'Where did you say you lived?' he asked Dad, irritably.

It had been two months since Dad moved out and Nick moved in. And Callum had seen his dad in town, been to the pictures and bowling and McDonald's with him. But had never been to his new house.

'I've rented a place,' said Dad. 'It's a little cottage, belonged to a Forestry Commission worker. It's right by a forest. You'll like it. You can climb trees and stuff.'

'Huh!' snorted Callum.

'You'll be able to see where I work in a minute,' said Dad. 'Not as well paid as the other job, but I was lucky to get it.'

Callum knew Dad had left his old job because of what had happened between Nick and Mum. Nick and Dad had worked for the same company. Mum had worked there too. And everything had seemed all right. Until two months ago when Callum's world was turned upside-down. And Nick moved in. And Dad moved out. Out of the house and out of the neighbourhood.

Callum was vague about what Dad had worked at before. He knew Dad and Mum were scientists, like Nick, and they did some kind of research for a big company. But he didn't know what the research was. He'd never asked—he wasn't really interested.

'There's the laboratories,' said Dad. 'It's a new company, Biogen. Only small—but doing some brilliant research. Real science fiction stuff, some of it.'

Callum yawned. He wasn't interested in this new job either. But when he did look out of the car window he couldn't help feeling a flicker of curiosity.

The laboratories were on a dark hillside. The building wasn't special—just a two-storey office block sort of place. But it was lit up like a prison camp, with a high wire fence and searchlights all around the perimeter. Tight security. Callum could see 'Keep out' signs on the fence.

'What goes on in there?' he asked Dad.

'Genetic engineering, to do with plants mainly. All sorts of projects. For instance, they're trying to make a new kind of fuel from plants for when oil runs out. An environmentally friendly fuel. Now that's really exciting stuff—I'd like to be involved in that. It's still experimental. And it's top secret. I'm not really supposed to be telling you about it.'

Callum gave his contemptuous snort again because he thought his dad was joking. He couldn't imagine him doing top secret work, like James Bond.

They were bumping down forest tracks now. There were no lights anywhere, except the car headlights. And they slid over gloomy pines whose branches brushed the car like searching arms. Once Callum caught a glimpse of golden eyes deep in the forest. He shivered. He didn't like this place. It was like the end of the world.

His fingers tightened round the box of matches in his pocket. He pulled it out, opened it. He took a sneaky glance at Dad. But he was busy concentrating on the twisty forest road.

Callum struck a match. It flashed blue in the dark and the tiny yellow flame was only small but it seemed to warm his heart.

He cupped it in his palm and watched it. The match burned lower. But Callum did not blow it out. He kept his hand steady. He didn't flinch, even when his flesh began to feel the heat. He was trying to see how much pain he could bear.

'What's that you're doing? Is something burning?'

Quickly, Callum pinched the match out with his fingers.

'Nothing. I'm not doing nothing. Don't you start blaming me as well!'

Callum's dad asked no more questions. But his eyes, as he watched his son through the driving mirror, were deeply troubled.

'We're here.'

Callum got out of the car, stretched his cramped legs. He took a deep breath. The air smelled of resin and pine needles. For the first time that night, he pulled off his hood.

He had a pleasant face, small and gnomish like his dad's. He had sharp blue eyes and a quick grin. Although the grin had not been used much lately.

'This is it,' said Dad.

All Callum saw was the front of a stone cottage. Everything else around them, the entire landscape, was swallowed up in darkness. Except, in the distance, there was a faint yellow halo of light above the trees. It was the security lights of Biogen, the genetic engineering company where Dad worked.

His dad was unlocking the front door of the house. Somewhere in the forest, an owl hooted.

''Course,' Dad was saying, 'the telly reception's terrible. It's because the trees are in the way. Sometimes you can't get a picture at all.'

'Oh, great,' muttered Callum, hunching his shoulders up so his neck disappeared into his jacket like a tortoise. 'That's just great. That's all I need.'

3

When Callum got up next morning Dad had already gone to work.

The little cottage was cramped. It had shabby furniture. And there was stuff everywhere—Mum had always hated Dad's untidiness. Clothes were slung on chairs, biology books were stacked on the table. On every window-sill was a jumble of fir cones, fossils, dried-up toadstools, and moss.

Dad had 'enthusiasms'. He was always finding something biological to be curious about. The trouble was, as Mum said, all Dad's enthusiasms made a lot of mess. Once, he had got interested in insects that breed in animal dung. And every day parcels of dried-up leopard dung and elephant dung and grizzly bear dung would arrive from all over the world. Until Mum had gone berserk. She had gone berserk, too, that time he put spiders in the fridge. Not to kill them, just to slow them down a bit so he could photograph them.

'But they're in test tubes,' Dad had protested. 'They can't escape.'

Mum had still gone berserk.

The latest enthusiasm was quite messy too. It left curly wood chips, like pencil shavings, all over the place. Dad had taken up carving birds and animals from bits of wood he found in the forest.

Callum didn't know Dad could carve things. He picked up a carving of a mandarin duck. He had to admit it was quite good. Callum stroked its smooth and polished body. It fitted snugly into the palm of his hand.

Dad had carved a badger too. He had tried a heron but one leg had snapped.

Callum put the duck down and wandered about, picking things up here and there. He made himself a tomato sauce sandwich. He ate an apple. He turned on the television. Just like Dad said, the reception was terrible. He could hardly see the picture. It was only black and white anyhow. Trust Dad to have a telly that belonged in the Stone Age! He punched the 'Off' button resentfully.

'It's boring here. There's nothing to do!' muttered Callum out loud. 'Dad didn't want me either. He didn't really want me here.'

Then, out of the blue, he thought of the matches in his coat pocket.

A demon seemed to take over his mind. He raced to his coat, plunged his hands in the pocket, scrabbled around. In his head a grotesque plan was hatching. He thought of the carvings—the mandarin duck, the badger, the one-legged heron. So patiently carved by his dad. He thought what a good blaze they would make piled in the empty grate, with the wood chips heaped around. Even as the idea sprang to life, his mind was revolted by it. But the demon seemed to goad him on. 'That'll show him,' the demon seemed to say. 'That'll make him take notice.'

But the matches were gone.

Feverishly Callum turned every pocket inside out. Crisp packets, chewing gum wrappers, his school bus pass, a detention slip. But no matches.

He's hidden them! thought Callum, outraged. He's gone and hidden them! What's he done that for? Doesn't he trust me?

Callum could have turned the cottage upside-down to find out where Dad had put the matches. But he didn't want them any more. Knowing that Dad was wise to him had, somehow, dumped cold water on the fire idea.

'Didn't want to do it anyhow,' Callum muttered to himself.

His restless eyes caught sight again of the sleek little mandarin duck. He was glad he hadn't had to burn it. He carried it over to the mantelpiece and put it up there, next to an old cracked teapot.

He wandered over to the window and peered out, even though he knew what he would see.

'Zillions of trees!' he told himself.

But what was really out there surprised him. He hadn't been able to see the landscape, last night in the dark.

The cottage was not slap-bang in the middle of a forest as Callum had thought. It was on moorland. Separated from the trees by half a mile of bracken and purple foxgloves. And the forest was not really a forest, but a small compact plantation of rows of dark green pines.

Outside there was bright sunshine.

'Suppose I'll have to go for a walk,' Callum decided, sighing. 'There's nothing else to do.'

He wouldn't have gone for a walk, he told himself, if there'd been anything else to do. Walking for walking's sake was uncool. He was glad his friends weren't here to see him.

He locked the cottage door behind him and put the key in the pocket of his jeans. Then, wrinkling his nose at the resiny, woodland smell, he set out for the plantation. He could hear the whine of chain saws. They were logging in there somewhere.

The bracken buzzed with tiny, emerald green flies. Callum tore off a bracken leaf and walked on, whipping it round his head to keep them off.

It was cool, green, less fly-infested among the pines. Sunlight dappled the path. A sudden gap in the trees opened up and, across the valley, Callum saw Dad's workplace. Biogen didn't look as sinister as it had in the dark. Callum wondered vaguely what Dad did inside that building. But it didn't occupy his mind for long.

He trudged on, swiping at gnats with his bracken leaf.

He was thinking now about Nick and how much he hated him. He was remembering the time when he first found out about Nick's Jekyll and Hyde character: when Nick spilled a mug of coffee on Mum's Chinese rug—and Callum saw him do it. And Mum found out and went berserk and said, looking at Callum, 'Who did this, as if I didn't know?' And Nick was standing there and said nothing, let Callum take the blame. And when Callum protested, Mum said to Nick, 'He did do it, didn't he?' And Nick put a finger to his lips and smiled as if he wouldn't tell. And Mum laughed and said, 'I can see you two are already best buddies. You're already ganging up against me!'

And afterwards, Nick had cornered Callum in the hallway and said, 'See that front door, sonny-boy? See that front door, you useless waste of space? In two years you'll be out of that door for good. You're nothing but trouble. In everybody's way. You know that, don't you?'

But Callum hadn't answered. He'd just stared back at Nick with a blank face and dead, expressionless eyes. He wouldn't give Nick the pleasure of seeing pain on his face. He'd practised that stony stare. Perfected it. He'd burnt down lots of matches trying to get it right.

One day, the burns on his hands were so bad that even Mum had taken notice.

'What's wrong with your hand?'

'Oh, nothing,' Callum had said, hiding it in his sleeve.

In his frustration, Callum gave a vicious kick to a stone lying on the forest path.

'Oi, watch what you're doing.'

Startled, Callum looked among the trees. At first he couldn't tell where the voice had come from. Rays of dusty sunlight dazzled him. He blinked and then he saw the logger. The logger was young with spiky red hair. He was standing near a tree he'd felled. His chain-saw lay idle at his feet.

'I'm just walking,' said Callum defensively. 'I'm not doing nothing wrong.'

'That's all right then.'

The logger wiped his hot face, sat down on the felled tree, took a swig from a bottle of water.

Callum was turning away when, by his left ear, came a loud, rattling buzz. He'd never heard anything like it before.

His head shot round. But the buzz had moved. He looked down.

A monster wasp, long and thick as his middle finger, had settled on his sleeve. It was striped black and bright, poison yellow. And it had a giant, whippy sting. Longer than its body. The sting was quivering.

Callum went wild. He flapped his arms, jigged about in a manic dance.

'Gerroff! Gerroff!' he roared.

He ran around among the trees, beating at his coat.

The logger sat calmly, eating his lunch. He unwrapped another cheese and tomato sandwich.

Callum came racing back. 'Has it gone?' There was nothing on his sleeve. 'Did you see it?' babbled Callum. 'This massive wasp. It was giant. This big! Did you see that sting? It was this big! It was—'

He heard the wasp first—that ferocious buzz. Then he saw it. Crawling over the felled tree-trunk the logger was sitting on. It stopped, to clean its long yellow antennae.

'Look out! Look out!' spluttered Callum. He pointed a shaking finger.

The logger looked casually down. 'You're not from round 'ere then?' he said to Callum.

And he flicked the wasp off the log. It writhed in the wood shavings. Dragged itself under the tree. Callum could hear its wounded buzzing.

'It's still alive!' he warned.

The logger shrugged. 'Don't matter. It can't hurt you anyway.'

'But what about that sting? It's this big! It could kill an elephant, that sting!'

'If it was a sting,' said the logger, chewing his sandwich. 'It isn't though. It's for laying eggs. That's a giant wood wasp. It can't hurt you. Ain't got no sting at all.'

Callum was silent. He shuffled his feet. He felt like a fool. 'Well, it looked dangerous,' he muttered, defensively.

Suddenly the logger startled him by leaping up, thrusting his hand into a tangle of torn branches.

'Gotcha!' he said.

He pulled his hand out. Dangling from it, by one leg, was a baby grey squirrel, screeching in fear. 'Thought there was a drey up there,' he said.

Callum went closer, curious about the wriggling creature. He wasn't particularly fond of animals. He didn't know much about them. His mum had never let him keep pets. She said they made a mess.

Callum asked, 'What you going to do with it?'

The logger shrugged. He seemed friendly, talkative. 'Kill it,' he explained to Callum. 'They're vermin—like rats. They do a lot of damage to trees. You always kill them when you get the chance.'

He changed his grip so his fingers squeezed the squirrel's neck.

'Ow, the little pest's bit me!'

The baby leapt. And landed, *splat*, flattened against Callum's T-shirt. It clung on desperately with its claws. Callum could feel them raking through the thin material.

But he clenched his teeth. He'd had plenty of practice at not showing pain. And he wasn't going to let the logger see him flinch. Not after he'd lost his cool over that wasp.

The logger grinned. 'It thinks you're its mum. Its mum won't come back for it. It'll die without her anyway. Kinder to kill it now.'

'Get it off me,' said Callum. But he kept his voice steady.

And then the squirrel, in one fluid movement, dived under his T-shirt. He saw its bushy tail whisk out of sight. Felt it scratching across his chest.

'Aargh! It's gone under my clothes!' cried Callum, squirming.

He'd gone and lost his cool again. In town, he hardly ever lost his cool. It must be something about the country.

'They do that,' said the logger, grinning, 'give 'em half a chance. It's just a baby 'un. Thinks it's safe, back in its nest.'

He moved towards Callum. 'Give it 'ere. I'll snap its neck for you, no trouble. Like I said, they're pests. No use to no one. Just a waste of space.'

Callum backed away, 'No!'

The squirrel had stopped moving. Callum squinted sideways, trying to see where it had gone. It was lying along his shoulder. He could feel it. Its tail was dangling from the sleeve of his T-shirt. He could see the tip poking out.

Carefully, Callum twisted his head round, lifted up the neck of his T-shirt and peered inside. The squirrel had fallen asleep, instantly, like a baby does, worn out by its alarm and distress. Fallen right to sleep, as if his shoulder was a branch, a safe place, high up in the tree top.

'You stupid baby squirrel,' Callum told it. But his voice was gentle. He felt a common bond with helpless, homeless creatures. Creatures that were a waste of space.

'Give it 'ere then,' said the logger. 'I 'aven't got all day.'

Callum backed off further, stumbling over fallen branches.

Then he turned and began to run, clumsily, with one shoulder hunched up so the squirrel didn't fall off.

He didn't look back. If he had done, he'd have seen that the logger didn't follow him. He just shrugged, shook his head.

'Not from round 'ere,' he said.

Then he picked up his chain-saw again. In seconds its angry snarl rose above the trees.

4

‘’Course,’ said Dad, ‘you know it’s illegal to keep them. And it’s illegal to let them go, as well. If you’ve got one, all you can legally do is kill it.’

‘No!’ said Callum, his eyes blazing defiance. ‘I’m going to keep it as a pet.’

‘You can’t,’ said Dad. ‘You can’t tame ’em. They’re too wild.’

‘Oh, come on, Dad,’ begged Callum. He held out his hand. The baby squirrel was fast asleep in his palm with its furry tail curled right around its body. It twitched in its sleep like a puppy.

‘It’s dreaming of trees,’ said Callum’s dad. ‘Dreaming of being right at the top of a high pine tree. You have to let it go.’

‘Not yet,’ said Callum. ‘The loggers’ll kill it. It’s just a baby. It’s lost its mum.’

Dad shrugged. ‘Keep it then,’ he said. ‘But you’ll soon see. It’s not as helpless as it looks. They’re related to rats. And rats are a very resourceful species. They’re real survivors. Rats could take over the world.’

‘It doesn’t look anything like a rat!’ protested Callum.

In the palm of his hand the baby squirrel looked harmless and helpless. Its ears had grey tufts on them. In its sleep the squirrel lifted a tiny pink paw and scratched its ear.

‘Aw, look at that,’ said Callum. ‘It’s really cute. It needs looking after . . . I’ll put it in my squirrel sweater.’

He had found the sweater in a heap of his dad’s clothes. It was big and baggy. And a perfect nesting place for squirrels.

It had a pouch pocket in the front and a hood at the back. All day Callum had been walking around wearing the squirrel sweater. And the squirrel had slept in it. Curled up behind his neck in the hood. Or inside the pouch, with its tail dangling out.

Callum had walked about very carefully, as if he were hatching eggs in his pockets.

And he had not thought of matches once. It was the first day for ages he had not tested his self-control by letting a match burn down to his skin. The trick was, to keep your face hard as stone. To show absolutely no emotion, even though you felt like whimpering with the pain.

Even the fire Dad had lit did not make his heart race, bring him out in a sweat of excitement as fires usually did. He was still fascinated by the flames. He gazed into them, seeing castles, dragons, roaring red waterfalls. But he felt quite calm. His heartbeat was normal.

'It's *my* squirrel sweater, actually,' Dad pointed out.

'Well, I'm only borrowing it! I haven't done nothing wrong!'

'OK, OK, it's all right!' soothed Dad. 'You can keep it. I don't mind. I'm on your side, remember. I like you!'

The fierce glitter went out of Callum's eyes. He grinned a quick, apologetic grin. Then slipped the squirrel inside the pouch pocket. It slept on. It had done nothing all day but sleep.

'It might not live,' warned Callum's dad, 'if it came crashing down with that tree. I'm surprised it's still alive. I'm surprised the shock didn't kill it.'

'Thought they were related to rats?' said Callum. 'Thought you said they were survivors?'

But his tone wasn't belligerent, as it almost always was with Nick. He felt oddly relaxed. Not spiky and defensive all the time. He was actually beginning to feel that the whole world wasn't against him.

Callum yawned, stretched back in one of Dad's busted armchairs. He felt as drowsy as his squirrel. Beyond the firelight the room was dark and mysterious, full of shifting shadows.

Dad was in a corner rummaging through piles of natural history books.

'Ah!' he cried. Pounced, dragged a book out: 'Knew I had this somewhere.'

He brought it nearer the fire so he could see it. 'This was written by an old bloke, lived in the country all his life.' He followed a line of print with his finger. '"If you want to keep squirrels as pets,"' he read out, '"then I have only one word of advice. Don't."'

'Why?' demanded Callum. 'Does he say why?'

Callum's dad scanned the rest of the page. 'Er . . . no,' he said. 'He just says don't.'

'Well, he's a stupid old git,' announced Callum, 'who doesn't know what he's talking about.'

He searched around for the half-finished bag of cheese and onion crisps he'd stuffed down the side of the chair. Prised them out and began, contentedly, to crunch them.

Suddenly, the room was flooded with harsh white light. It came from outside the window. Callum blinked, dazzled.

'What's that?'

Dad put down the book. Went over to the window and tried to squint out through the glare.

He turned back. 'Car headlights,' he said. 'There's a car out there. Shining its lights at the house. Must be somebody lost. Some stranger. These back roads are like a maze. They all look the same in the dark.' He opened the front door. 'I'll go and see.'

Callum didn't move. He was too comfortable, toasting his socks in the warmth of the fire. He must have dozed off because when he woke up the car headlights had gone. And Dad was shaking him, roughly, by the shoulder.

Callum stared at him with wide, astonished eyes. 'Hey, what you doing? Hey, mind my squirrel!'

He thought Dad was playing some kind of joke.

But it was no joke. Dad's face was twisted with distress. 'You told me you never set fire to things before. You told me it was the first time!'

'I never did!' roared Callum. 'Well, only little fires. Litter bins and stuff. That doesn't count.'

'Only little fires! What about the school you set fire to?'

'What school? What you talking about?' Callum wriggled out of his father's grasp. He lunged to his feet. In his pocket the baby squirrel woke up. It began to squirm frantically, inside the pouch. It couldn't find its way out.

Callum had forgotten all about it. As he jigged about in angry frustration, the baby squirrel clung on, screeching, inside the pouch. It remembered being safe in its nest in the high tree top. And then the nest shaking. And the safe world crashing down in noise and panic and confusion.

'I never set fire to no school,' Callum bawled at his dad. 'What you blaming me for?' He made his voice surly, resentful, just as if he were talking to Nick. Then he said, 'You're just like him. Just like that bastard, Nick. He's always blaming me for something!'

'Well, maybe he was right! Maybe he was right to think you're trouble! Maybe there's a lot about you I didn't know!'

Callum's dad regretted these words as soon as they escaped from his mouth. But by then it was far too late.

Callum's jaw dropped. The expression in his eyes was appalled disbelief. It was as if his dad had betrayed him.

He fought to reply. But he couldn't seem to make proper words. He could only choke and stutter.

In the end, he raced off to his bedroom, clashing his head on the low beams, bashing himself against walls. In his pocket the baby squirrel's thin, high-pitched screams went on and on, unnoticed.

Callum lay on his bed, trembling and muttering to himself. He was saying 'bastard', over and over again. And this time he meant Dad, not Nick. He'd thought Dad was on his side. He'd said so, hadn't he? He'd thought that, whoever turned against him, at least his own dad would still stand up for him.

'Some chance,' Callum sneered at himself. 'What did you expect? He just let Nick move in, didn't he? And what did he do? He just moved out! Let Nick take over. He's useless he is. He's got no guts!'

He scrabbled under the pillow for his matches. That was where he kept them at home. But then he remembered he wasn't at home. He was stuck here, out in the wilds, with fuzzy television reception, in a landscape where the pine tree was king. No McDonald's, no video shops, no supermarkets. It felt as alien as Mars.

He did wonder, briefly, why Dad had got worked up all of a sudden. And about fires too. Callum had persuaded himself the subject of fires was closed. Forgiven and forgotten.

I mean, we were getting on great, thought Callum, with a baffled shake of his head. Then he starts yelling at me! And accusing me of all sorts of stuff!

But just as his mind was getting to grips with this mystery, he felt a soft tail brush his face.

'Squirrel!' cried Callum joyfully, as if he was greeting his only friend in the world.

The squirrel, calmer now, looked back at him with shining, curious eyes. There was no suspicion in those eyes. They seemed to trust him, totally.

Callum groped down by the bed. He was sure there were peanuts on the floor somewhere. He held one out between his finger and thumb.

The squirrel took it daintily in its little needle teeth. It tried to balance, fanning out its tail like a fern leaf, arching it over its head. It fell over, rolled in a ball, lost the nut.

Callum smiled. The smile muscles of his face felt stiff, as if he hadn't used them for a long time.

'You've got to practise,' Callum said. 'Practise being a squirrel.'

He held out the nut again.

As if it understood him, the squirrel grasped the nut in its paws, fluffed out its tail. This time it didn't fall over. It perched on Callum's chest, gobbling the nut like a tiny shredding machine, turning it round and round in frantic hands. It was a manic, messy eater. Bits of nut sprayed all over the duvet.

Callum gave it another. It demolished it in a blur of teeth and claws and debris.

'Wow!' Callum was impressed. He flicked a speck of nut off his nose.

Already his pet was beginning to look less like a cuddly toy and more like a rodent. It seemed leaner, sleeker, bolder. Less easy to handle. It was growing up very fast.

Callum chain-fed his squirrel peanuts. Until, cram-full of them, it stored the last few away in the pouch pocket—for later.

Then it nosed its way back into the pocket. It fell asleep instantly, like switching off a light.

Callum stroked the silky fur of the squirrel's tail.

'That guy didn't like you. He said you were a waste of space. He said you were vermin. Well, I don't think you're vermin,' murmured Callum to the sleeping squirrel, before he too fell asleep.

5

As soon as Callum woke up next morning he felt uneasy. He felt he had gone to sleep with a problem on his mind. Not an old problem, but a fresh new problem, demanding his urgent attention.

Then he remembered the row he'd had with Dad. How they'd been getting on brilliantly. Then Dad had gone outside, to help strangers find their way in the forest. And had come back later—Callum had dozed off so wasn't sure how much later—like a bear with a sore head. Yelling about fires and making all sorts of wild accusations.

'What's he want to go on about fires for?' muttered Callum reproachfully. 'I've given all that up.'

It was true that only last night his fingers had itched for a match. But that was only to test his own strength, to see if he could stand the pain without flinching. He hadn't intended to start a blaze or anything like that.

He listened. The house was very quiet. Looked at his watch—8.30. Dad had already left for work.

When he got off the bed a shower of peanut crumbs fell from the squirrel sweater.

'You messy animal,' Callum informed the squirrel. 'Come on, you lazy squirrel, wake up.'

The sweater was beginning to smell a bit. It was bound to, with a squirrel's nest inside it. But Callum wasn't going to take it off. Not so long as Squirrel thought of it as home.

He prodded the pouch pocket. The squirrel wasn't there.

'Where's he gone?' muttered Callum to himself. He looked round the tiny room. The only thing in it besides his bed was a chair, with his jeans slung over the back. Nowhere for a squirrel to hide. Callum checked under the bed, just in case. He shook out the bedclothes. No squirrel.

In his bare feet, wearing boxer shorts and the squirrel sweater, Callum went padding down the stairs into the living room. He felt a fool calling, 'Squirrel! Squirrel!' his voice growing more desperate by the second.

A squirrel could hide out forever in this clutter. Callum shifted a few books, rummaged among the heaps of Dad's clothes. He picked out a pair of Dad's jogging pants, put them on. They concertinaed round his legs. But Callum didn't mind that. He liked his clothes baggy.

'Squirrel! Squirrel!'

There were stripped pine cones on the window-sill—and brown flakes all over the floor. The shredding machine had been at work. Callum bent down to inspect this clue, straightened up again.

He's around here somewhere, he thought, relieved.

Whump! A furry missile clamped itself like Alien to his face. Callum staggered back, wearing a squirrel mask. His arms beat the air. He was suffocating. The squirrel was hugging his mouth, nose, and eyes, clinging on grimly with tiny claws hooked into his flesh.

'Gerroff!' shrieked Callum. 'Gerroff!'

He reached up to wrench the squirrel off his face. It was like detaching an octopus. Every time he pulled claws loose they clutched, like tentacles, at something else. His hair, his ear, even his eyelid. And all the time Squirrel screeched in protest.

At last Callum plucked it off. It squirmed out of his hand, raced down his leg.

'No!'

Too late. Callum saw its tail whisking up his baggy trousers.

'Aargh!' He doubled up in anticipation. But the squirrel scampered lightly up his leg, dived out of the top of his trousers and into the pouch pocket. It left its tail, as usual, dangling on the outside. And went to sleep, as if nothing had happened.

'Phew!' said Callum. He eased himself into a chair. 'That could've been nasty.'

For a moment he felt a familiar burning resentment. As if the squirrel had a grudge against him. As if it had hurt him deliberately. The scratches on his face were stinging like mad. He reached up and touched one.

'Ow!'

It had really scared him. When the squirrel suckered itself to his face he had felt blind, choking panic.

He glared down at the bushy tail.

It twitched. The squirrel was probably dreaming of peanuts, of pine cones and sun-dappled woods. It felt safe with him, protected, as if it was in a nest.

And, suddenly, Callum's anger just fizzled out, scattered like sparks on the wind. He even found himself grinning.

'It just thought you were a tree,' he told himself, shrugging. 'It's a squirrel, isn't it? It's just doing what squirrels do.'

Just practising essential squirrel skills, he decided. Taking mad flying leaps, clinging on for dear life, scuttling up and down tree trunks. It hadn't meant to hurt him. Nothing personal. It was just doing what squirrels do.

He got up carefully from the chair and went into the kitchen. There, by the big bottle of Coca Cola, where he knew Callum would find it, Dad had left him a peace-offering.

Callum stared at it. It was a carving, in honey-coloured wood, of Squirrel asleep. The way it slept in the palm of Callum's hand, curled up like a snail, with its tail wrapped right round its body and its paws tucked up by its nose.

Callum picked up the carving. It fitted into his hand, smooth and round as a sea-washed pebble.

It was beautiful—made specially for him. Dad must have stayed up all night to do it.

Callum was touched. He wished Dad were here now, so he could say thanks.

I'll go and meet him tonight, thought Callum. I'll meet him from work. Say thanks straight away.

He put the carving on the mantelpiece, next to the mandarin duck and the cracked teapot.

Callum thought the hours would drag. But he had no time to clockwatch. Squirrel proved to be a real handful. Overnight, it seemed, it had changed from a helpless baby into a hyperactive tearaway.

It woke up. It was off. Dashing up curtains, shredding nuts, making crazy leaps from Callum to the curtains to the mantelpiece, back to Callum again. It ran up his trouser legs, along his arms. His sweater bulged like Popeye's muscles. It scrabbled in plant pots like a dog digging up bones. Soil sprayed everywhere—the carpet was gritty with it. It demolished Dad's geraniums. Took them up to the curtain rail and minced them in its little ratty teeth. Petals came showering down like red confetti.

Callum was run off his feet, his head in a spin. All day he chased it round the house, trying to stop it wrecking the place.

'It's just being a squirrel,' he reminded himself, breathlessly. 'Just doing what squirrels do.'

He tried to coax it down off the curtains. It chattered at him angrily. He tried to stop it chewing the chair legs. It shot him a bright, delinquent stare and rushed up the curtains again.

'Come down here, you menace!' said Callum. 'Behave yourself; we've got to go in a minute.'

But the squirrel was a wild, wild creature, a law unto itself. It took no notice at all of what it was told.

'Don't!' had been the countryman's advice to people who tried to domesticate squirrels.

Can see what he means, thought Callum as he shook geranium petals out of his hair.

Callum gave up. He slumped in a chair. It was four o'clock. Time to make a move if he wanted to meet Dad from work.

'I'll have to go without you,' Callum warned the squirrel.

Then, to his amazement, Squirrel came down from the curtains. It crept into the pocket of his squirrel sweater. Callum waited for it to bounce out again, as if it was on elastic. But it didn't. He peeped inside. It was curled up into a ball, just like the carving Dad had made. Its eyes were closed. It looked peaceful as a sleeping baby.

'About time too,' Callum told it. 'You're nothing but trouble.'

Callum took the carving with him. When he picked it up from the mantelpiece he saw a box of matches, wedged behind the teapot.

So that's where he's hidden them, thought Callum.

He was going to leave them there. Then he changed his mind. He stuffed them into his coat pocket—just in case.

Callum locked the house. With a wooden squirrel tucked in the palm of his hand and real-life squirrel in his pocket he set off to walk to Biogen to meet his dad.

'You're Squirrel Boy,' Callum told himself with a wry grin. It didn't sound very cool. Wolf Boy or Dolphin Boy or something, that would've been OK. But Squirrel Boy?

The shortest way was through the plantation, through the green shade of the pines. Callum kept an eye open for the red-haired logger. Being Squirrel Boy might not be cool, but he had rescued this squirrel from certain death. There was no way Red-hair was going to get his hands on it.

There were people in the plantation, bombing about on mountain bikes, picnicking at wooden tables.

Callum passed a sedate group of old people, picnicking. They had fold-up chairs and a hamper and a red-checked cloth on a table.

In the pocket of the squirrel sweater something stirred.

'Oh no,' groaned Callum. 'Go back to sleep.'

But Squirrel was born to be wild. He had a sudden burst of manic activity. He sprang out of the pocket, down Callum's leg and began to rip up the grass round his feet. He was digging for juicy roots.

An old lady spotted him first. With cries of delight the whole picnic party turned to stare.

'Oh look, a squirrel!'

'How sweet!'

'He's just a baby!'

'Isn't he cute?'

Squirrel dived up Callum's trouser leg.

The picnic party gasped.

Callum looked unconcerned. As if a squirrel up your trouser leg is something that happens every day. Nothing to get worked up about.

'It's gone up his trousers!'

The squirrel emerged through the neck of Callum's sweater. It whisked round his throat like a furry boa then shot down his sleeve, making bulging biceps on the way.

The picnic party goggled, bug-eyed.

Squirrel Boy whistled casually. He just kept right on walking. Real cool. Apparently indifferent to a wild creature doing circuit training under his clothing.

The squirrel thrust its nose out of his cuff. Too tight. It wriggled back. Dashed up his sleeve, down his chest and back into the pouch pocket.

It fell asleep.

But by then Callum was back among the trees. Leaving the picnic party in stunned silence. Their mouths slack with astonishment.

Biogen was just down the road. Beyond the high security fence, Callum could see Dad's old wreck of a car in the car park.

He sat down to wait in the shade of a hedge. It was very quiet. He could hear mice squeaking through grassy tunnels all around him.

Five o'clock. Cars began to drive out of Biogen. Past the security man in his glass cubicle. He didn't look very tough for a security man, decided Callum. He was wearing a smart blue uniform, but he was too old and too fat. You could easily outrun him.

Callum waited. Several cars drove out. Each time the security man raised a barrier so they could get out. Then they drove straight through the main gates, which stood open. Soon, only Dad's car was left in the park.

Callum waited some more. He was getting restless. He hated waiting. But, more than that, he was anxious to make it up with Dad, to thank him for the carving.

The security man was looking at Dad's car. He picked up a phone in the glass cubicle, talked into it. Then Callum watched as he left the cubicle and disappeared into the building. There was no one on guard.

'I'm sick of waiting,' muttered Callum to himself. He made a decision. He would go and see what Dad was doing. Maybe he's working late, thought Callum.

He checked the squirrel. Still asleep, probably worn out after its wrecking spree.

And then he walked across the road, in through the main gates and ducked under the barrier.

'Easy,' shrugged Callum to himself.

He didn't feel worried. If anyone challenged him, he had his story ready. He would just look innocent and say he was looking for his dad. It wasn't even a lie.

He'd planned to walk straight into the building. But he couldn't get in. There was some sort of security lock on the main doors where you had to punch in your number. He peered through the glass doors. All he could see was a corridor—long and white, like a hospital corridor—with some doors leading off it. No signs of life at all.

'Where are you, Dad?' fumed Callum. It annoyed him that his dad was making him wait, when he'd come all this way on a peace-making mission. It was almost as if Dad was doing it deliberately.

Callum scowled. The matches rattled in his pocket. For a second, he yearned to take them out.

The yearning passed.

Instead, he roamed round the building, peering in windows, trying to find Dad. But all he saw were empty laboratories. They all looked the same. Long white tables, masses and masses of glass bottles on shelves, computers, microscopes. There were warning signs everywhere—ACCESS RESTRICTED signs and lots of black triangles on a yellow background, with a sort of black propeller inside them. Callum knew what they were. They were bio-hazard signs. His dad had brought some home once, from the last place where he'd worked with Nick and Mum. And Callum had stuck them all over his bedroom door.

He moved along to the next window. Someone there. But it wasn't the fat security man.

It didn't even look human. It looked alien—or android. Dressed all in white: white coat, white boots, white gloves. The face was masked and the head completely covered by a white hood. Even the eyes, which might have reassured you it was human, were hidden behind some kind of protective shield.

Instinctively, Callum dropped down so only his eyes were visible above the window-sill. Squatting on his heels, he carried on watching.

On the far wall of the lab was what looked to Callum like a white refrigerator. It was smothered with bio-hazard warnings. And it also said, in giant red letters: THIS INCUBATOR STRICTLY OFF LIMITS TO NON-AUTHORIZED PERSONNEL.

White android crouched by the incubator. His movements seemed to Callum sneaky, hurried. He kept glancing towards the lab door. There was a full length glass panel in the lab door. Callum could see through it, to the white corridor outside.

It wasn't empty. Right at the end of it, just turning the corner, was someone in a blue uniform, the security man.

But from where he crouched, white android couldn't see him.

White android opened the incubator. He stretched a gloved hand into it. The security man came down the corridor. He was unlocking doors, checking rooms. Getting nearer and nearer.

The hand came out with a clear plastic Petri dish. The lid was taped on. Callum frowned. He could see nothing inside it—except some kind of neon-pink jelly. White android slipped the flat dish into his lab coat pocket. Then, from his left hand pocket he took another Petri dish. To Callum it looked identical. Clear plastic, bright-pink jelly. He slipped the dish into the incubator. Carefully closed the door. Looked up.

Just as the security man put his bloodshot eye to the glass panel. He didn't unlock it. He didn't seem to have a pass-key for this laboratory. Instead his eye swivelled round, checking the inside. The hooded figure ducked back behind the incubator.

Callum licked dry lips. His eyes flickered anxiously from the security guard to white android. He didn't know whose side he was on. Usually security guards weren't his favourite people—the ones in the shopping mall seemed to have a grudge against him. They watched him like hawks. But this one was flabby and breathless. He didn't stand a chance. He would be helpless against white android. Perhaps the android had special powers, thought Callum. Perhaps, he thought wildly, he could suck your brains out down your nose with one gloved finger. He had seen a film where aliens could do that.

'Stop it,' Callum ordered his fevered brain. But he hardly dared look. He closed his eyes tight. When he opened them again the guard had gone. Callum could see him retreating, flat-footed, down the corridor.

White android came slowly out of his hiding place. He stood up. He wasn't as tall as Callum had expected.

He put his hands to his head. He was about to take off his hood. Callum held his breath. He half-expected to see some hideous mutant face under that disguise. He'd seen films like that too.

But when the hood came off he saw that white android had no special powers. None at all.

6

For a few seconds Callum clung on to the window-sill, stunned, gazing into the lab. Nothing there. The white android had vanished. As if it was no more real than a hologram.

But there was no denying his dad's face. That had been real all right. He could see it now, as the white hood slid off. It had been grey with strain and fear. Callum had never seen Dad look like that before.

For a few seconds he crouched there, frozen. Inside his mind was a whirling confusion. But he couldn't seem to move his legs at all.

Then, through the glass panel in the lab doors, he saw the security man cross the end of the corridor. He was heading for the exit. As soon as he left the building, he would see Callum spying through a window.

Run! Callum's brain shrieked at him. Run!

Callum sprinted across the car park. He'd always been a good runner—it had saved his skin more than once.

He dived under the barrier, out of the main gates and hurled himself into the long grass by the roadside.

Panting, he poked his head above trembling grass stems. Dived down again. Just in time. The security guard was back in his little glass box.

'You don't have to hide,' Callum reminded himself. 'You're not doing nothing wrong. You're just waiting for your dad.'

Defiantly, he got to his knees, then his feet. He was in full view. But if the security guard saw him, he made no sign. He picked up a folded newspaper, began doing the crossword.

'You're not doing nothing wrong,' Callum reassured himself again. 'You're not even trespassing.'

And what about Dad? Had he done something wrong?

'Come on,' Callum reasoned with himself. 'He was just working late, that's all. Maybe he didn't want to talk to that security man. He looks like a boring old fart.'

But Callum could have sworn that the white android was up to no good—sneaking about, hiding from security men. Taking a dish from an incubator, swapping it with an identical one . . .

A long limp tail uncurled, flopped out of the squirrel sweater.

I've crushed him! thought Callum, in sudden panic.

When he flung himself flat in the grass just now he'd forgotten Squirrel. With shaking hands he opened the pouch pocket, slid one hand inside, eased Squirrel out on the flat of his palm. As if his palm were a tiny stretcher.

Squirrel's body was light as a feather—a puff of Callum's breath could have blown it away.

Squirrel's eyes were sealed tight.

'Oh no,' groaned Callum.

Then Squirrel twitched, scratched its ear. Opened one bright eye. There was mayhem in that eye.

Callum laughed out loud with relief. 'You're all right!'

Instantly Squirrel was all systems go. It scuttled up to Callum's shoulder, perched there like a parrot, shredding a nut from its hoard in the squirrel sweater. Callum knew he would have to rake out his ear afterwards to get rid of the nut crumbs. But this time, he didn't mind at all.

'You gave me a real fright,' he told the squirrel sternly. 'You're nothing but trouble!'

In the Biogen car park Dad's car slid out of its parking space.

Callum's gaze darted over to it. He watched as it slowed down by the barrier. Dad got out of the car, shared a joke with the security man. He was smiling. The security man was smiling. If there was anything wrong, Callum couldn't see it.

Dad was dressed in his normal clothes: jeans, hiking boots, faded blue T-shirt. This one had a hare on it. Dad had a liking for T-shirts with wildlife motifs. He had a dolphin one, an otter one, even one with a herd of elephants on it. He sent away for them from wildlife magazines. They'd caused Callum a lot of embarrassment in the past—they were seriously uncool.

But now all he thought was, Come on, Dad. Hurry up, get out of there.

He couldn't shake off a chill of unease. Couldn't forget the moment when white android had lifted its hood. And there was Dad's face, sick and scared, underneath.

Callum waved, walked out into the bright sunlight of the road.

Dad drove straight at him. Callum had to dive out of the way. Squirrel, clinging frantically to his shoulder, chattered like an angry chimp.

'Dad!' yelled Callum.

The car screeched to a halt.

Callum ran up to it, climbed in.

'You nearly ran me over. Didn't you see me? I was right in front of you!'

Dad turned strange, far-away eyes on Callum. He didn't look mad, as he had last night. He looked dazed, as if he was in shock.

When he spoke, his voice seemed distant, mechanical. 'Where did you spring from?'

'I was waiting,' said Callum. 'I've been waiting for ages.'

Should he confess what he'd seen? It was on the tip of his tongue. But, suddenly, he decided not to. Not yet, anyway.

Instead he said, casually, 'What were you doing in there? I thought you were never going to get out! Everyone else went ages ago.'

Dad flinched, as if at some private memory. Callum had to repeat the question.

'What took you so long?'

Dad jerked to attention, as if he'd just noticed Callum was in the car.

'Er . . . just something I had to do.'

Then his eyes took on that odd, distant stare. He was looking out of the windscreen. But he didn't seem to see the road ahead.

Callum shrugged. 'Come on, then, let's get going.'

Dad said, 'What are those scratches on your face?'

'Squirrel did them,' said Callum. 'But he didn't mean it.'

'Good job your tetanus jabs are up to date,' said Dad vaguely, as if he was thinking about something else.

He started up the car. They drove off, down the road, turned left along a track into the plantation.

Callum was surprised to find he felt safer amongst the trees.

'I came to meet you,' explained Callum. 'To say sorry for last night. We got mad at each other, remember?'

He looked hard at Dad's face. But he couldn't tell whether he was listening or not.

'And I came,' said Callum, 'to say thank you for the squirrel you carved. It was really good. Must have taken ages.'

As he spoke about the carving, he was searching for it in his pockets. Matches in that one—he snatched his hand out before they rattled, gave him away—but no carving. He poked his hand in the squirrel's nest. The squirrel nipped his fingers for invading its territory.

'Ow!' protested Callum.

But he'd found the carving. Except, when he pulled it out, Squirrel had notched it all round with his tiny teeth. Spoiled those smooth curves. He'd been trying to open it, like a nut.

'Oh no,' said Callum. 'He's ruined it. Look, Dad, he's put toothmarks all over it.' He felt upset and angry, as if the squirrel had done it deliberately.

He thrust the carving under Dad's nose, as he was driving. 'Look what he's done!'

Dad glanced down briefly. 'I'll make you another,' he said in that flat, lifeless voice.

Then he seemed to wake up. 'What have you been doing today?' he demanded, with sudden urgency. 'Have you been behaving yourself?'

''Course I have,' protested Callum, instantly defensive. 'I'm not a little kid!'

'No more fires?' said Dad. 'You didn't find the matches, did you?'

'What are you talking about fires for?' Callum exploded. In his pocket, his fingers curled round the box of matches. 'I thought we were going to forget about that? I told you, didn't I, I was only messing about. I didn't mean to hurt Nick. I won't do it again. How many times do I have to tell you? Can't we just forget about it now? Can't we just pretend it never happened?'

'I wish we could,' muttered Dad grimly, as they pulled up in front of the house.

All evening, Dad was in the strangest mood. Callum couldn't make sense of it. One minute he seemed to be on a different planet. You spoke and he didn't answer. The next minute he was all nerves—his ears sensitive as radar. Every sound made him twitch.

The squirrel irritated him. It was having one of its crazy half-hours, behaving like a kid let loose in an adventure playground. It sped up the curtains. Made a death-defying leap from the curtain rail to Callum's head. Then dashed up the curtains and did it again. And again and again, until it made you dizzy to watch him.

'You'll have to let that squirrel go in the wild,' said Dad. 'It doesn't belong in a house. It has to learn to fend for itself.'

'I can't do that,' said Callum, alarmed. 'Not yet. It's still a baby! It needs looking after.'

But even Callum had to admit that Squirrel didn't behave like a helpless baby. Its eyes glittered with fierce independence. Every hour, it seemed, its climbing and leaping stunts got bolder, more skilful. It didn't look like a baby either. It looked like a rat with a big bushy tail.

Nothing wrong with rats, thought Callum defensively. Rats are very intelligent.

But he knew he'd have to let Squirrel go. It was wrecking the place. Soon, it would gnaw the furniture to matchwood.

But, 'It still needs me,' he told himself. He hated to think of Squirrel, abandoned in the forest. He remembered those mad golden eyes; those whispering, sighing pines. The forest got spooky, after dark. He wouldn't like to be out there, all alone.

Burr, burr! The telephone.

Callum's dad seemed to go into spasm. His whole body shook. His face went deathly white. He looked as if he was going to be sick.

'Shall I answer it?' asked Callum.

'No!'

Dad staggered for the door.

Callum looked after him, bewildered. What the hell's going on? he was thinking. What's wrong with him?

Dad came back after thirty seconds. He looked pale, but more in control.

'I have to go out,' he said to Callum.

'Where?' said Callum. He made it sound like a challenge.

'Er . . . er . . . I have to pop back to Biogen. That was the security bloke. I've left an electron microscope on. Got to go and turn it off.'

Callum knew Dad was lying. When Nick lied, he was so smooth, so glib. He looked straight into your eyes. He was a very good liar.

But Dad was the world's worst liar. He stuttered. He couldn't look at you. And he always gave up and told you the truth in the end.

But this time he didn't do that. He said, 'I won't be long.' And he shrugged on his coat and ducked out of the door before Callum could ask any more questions.

Callum stared through the window. Darkness had fallen but it was bright as day out there with a high moon and a clear sky speckled with stars. Dad didn't take the car. Why didn't he take the car? Instead he began walking through foxgloves and bracken towards the forest.

Callum followed him. He was pretty sure by now that Dad was in some kind of trouble. He plucked Squirrel off the curtains and stuffed him into the squirrel sweater. He rammed a handful of peanuts after him.

Squirrel chattered in protest but stayed put.

Callum slipped through the ghostly, blue-grey landscape. He tried to keep his dad in sight but it was hard. He kept melting into shadows.

A bramble branch snared Callum's foot. He staggered, almost fell. When he freed his foot, Dad had disappeared amongst the pines.

'Lost him,' muttered Callum.

He too plunged into the plantation.

His feet rustled in dry pine needles, squelched on fungus.

He stood still for a moment. Pine trunks, in lines like soldiers, stretched away in all directions. Vanished into darkness. Above his head branches creaked and whispered. Callum listened. Nothing but the branches talking. And tiny furtive scuttlings in the undergrowth.

Then he heard human voices. Off to his right.

He crept closer. The voices stopped.

'Shhh!' he commanded Squirrel, who was having a snack in his pocket. In that silence, Squirrel's peanut-munching seemed as loud as a dog crunching bones.

Squirrel, of course, paid no attention. He never did what he was told. He was born to be wild.

Callum frowned. Carried on creeping. The voices started up again.

'So what name have they given it? Their new bug?' said one voice. Callum's whole body stiffened. He knew that voice!

'*Pyrobacter*,' said a second voice. The second voice was just as familiar. But it was subdued, deadly serious. '*Pyrobacter liquifaciens*. But you know the score, Nick. This bacterium hasn't had safety checks yet. Hasn't been cleared for release. I can't tell you how stable it is. I've tried to find out but I'm not part of that research team—and information's restricted.'

Callum peered through a filter of spiky branches. He saw Nick and Dad standing in a moonlit clearing, beside a rack of twiggy brooms, used to beat out forest fires. Nick's car was parked a little way down the track.

'No problem,' said Nick. 'I'm not about to release it. And I can probably tell you more about it than they can.'

Dad had just handed over the Petri dish. Nick laid it on his palm, gazed through the taped-on lid into the pink jelly. Carried on talking. Nick liked to talk. He could run rings round you just by talking.

'I want to look at it back at the lab, that's all. See how far they've got. Like I said, I know I'm well ahead in the race. So you're not giving anything away—Biogen won't lose out. I just like to know what the opposition's up to. There's high stakes here. Fuel from plants! I mean any plant, not just sugar cane. It's a dream result. Cheap, efficient, environmentally friendly. We'll all be running our cars on it soon. And all you need to do it is a little bug, just a bit smarter than the one that's growing in here. Whoever patents it first is going to make millions.'

'And you'll destroy this bacterium, afterwards?' asked Callum's dad. 'Like you said?'

'Sure,' said Nick casually. 'What would I want with it? It's primitive compared to what I've got. My research was at this stage, maybe a year, two years ago. It's no use to me—except to know how far ahead I am. And take it from me, I'm a long, long way ahead.'

'I didn't even know you were working on this sort of thing,' said Dad.

Nick laughed. He smoothed down his beard. 'Well,' he said, 'you didn't know about a lot of things, did you, old buddy?'

Callum was listening to Nick talk and talk. But the words were going right over his head. He was too shocked, too horrified to take them in. The sight of his dad and Nick together meant only one thing to him. Nick was at his sly tricks again. Poisoning Dad's mind against him. Getting Dad on his side, just like he'd got Mum. Callum couldn't believe it. He believed many bad things about his dad—that he was a wimp, that he'd given in to Nick too easily. But he'd never, ever believed that Dad would gang up with Nick against him. Yet here they were, deep in secret conversation. As if they were in league with each other. Callum never doubted that their conversation was about him.

He clenched his fists in anguish. He felt everyone was against him. And that he was alone, out in the cold.

He would have headbutted the nearest tree. But he had to keep his desperation quiet. He fumbled for his matches. He needed to set the world ablaze.

Where were they? He groped in the pouch pocket. Squirrel gave him a vicious nip.

'Ow!' Callum snatched his hand out, sucked at a bead of blood. Had they heard him? He peered anxiously through the screen of branches.

Dad was saying, in a quiet, grim voice, 'Just remember your side of the bargain.'

'Trust me,' said Nick, in that half-mocking, half-serious way he had of speaking. 'My lips are sealed. No hard feelings?'

For a second, Callum thought Dad was going to hit Nick. He almost burst out from his hiding place, yelling, 'Go on, Dad, thump 'im! He deserves it!'

But Dad didn't thump Nick. Instead he turned abruptly away, strode across the clearing, disappeared into the trees.

Callum watched Nick's handsome, bearded face. And he saw Nick smile.

Callum's eyes narrowed. He began to circle round, still hidden by the trees. Circle round to where Nick was standing.

He didn't know what he was going to do. Anger drove him, burning in his throat like fire. He felt the whole world was against him now. And he blamed Nick for it. He blamed Nick for everything.

Nick began walking back towards his car. Callum quickened his steps.

He was very close. His shoe cracked a twig. Nick's head whipped round.

'Aaargh!'

Nick was shrieking, staggering about, clawing at his face.

He dropped the Petri dish. Callum didn't see that. He didn't see Nick's heel crush the dish either. What he did see, in quick-fire scenes like fast-forwarding a video, was Squirrel hooked on to Nick's face. Saw Nick twirl like a frantic dancer. Crash against his car. Bounce off in a blind panic.

His hands groped upwards. He tore Squirrel from his face. Flung him away like a rag.

Callum saw blood on Nick's forehead. Dripping from his ear lobe. But he didn't feel any satisfaction. He wasn't interested in Nick any longer.

Nick fell into his car. It roared into life. Went swerving away, the headlights slashing wild arcs through the trees.

Callum heard it go. But he was on his knees by then, scraping through the pine needles.

'C'mon, boy! Where are you, boy?'

His voice sounded very lonely and scared among those high pines, in the whispering dark.

'I'll kill that Nick,' sobbed Callum, 'if he's hurt my squirrel. I'll kill him—I will, I'll bloody well kill him.'

But then, with a soft, furry plop, something landed on his chest. Callum looked down.

'Squirrel!'

Squirrel had returned. He had not deserted Callum. He was tough. He was indestructible. It seemed he could survive anything. He gave Callum a quick, indifferent glance then whisked into the pouch pocket. You could hear him in there, shredding peanuts.

'It's just you and me, Squirrel,' said Callum. 'Just you and me,' as if Squirrel were his only friend in the world.

7

Callum jogged back through the moonlit wood.

He was going to confront his dad. Demand an explanation.

Seeing Nick and Dad together had completely wrecked his cool. His heart was bursting with the shock and pain of it. His mind was a whirlpool of wild suspicions.

He was so frantic that, if you'd handed him a match, he wouldn't even have stopped to light it.

He had his accusations ready. He rehearsed them as he ran.

'I saw you!' he'd yell as soon as he got back. 'Having secret meetings. Making some kind of deal with that sneaky bastard. How can you even talk to him? I told you what he's like!'

Squirrel clung on tight. He got bounced about. Didn't fall—he could cling to tree-tops in high winds.

Claws like tiny grappling hooks tugged at Callum's skin. But he didn't mind. Because Squirrel was on his side. The only one left on his side.

'You showed that Nick,' muttered Callum. 'You really showed him.'

And he thought, with grim satisfaction, of Nick stumbling about with Squirrel hanging off his face.

He didn't want to believe that when Squirrel leapt on Nick he was only practising his tree-top jumps. So he didn't believe it. Instead he convinced himself that Squirrel attacked Nick deliberately. For his sake.

'You got more guts than Dad,' Callum told Squirrel. 'At least you stood up for me.'

His voice was very bitter.

He charged into the cottage, blood boiling, spoiling for a fight. His mouth wide open to start yelling.

He stopped, confused. The room was dark. Callum felt for the light switch.

Dad was sitting in the busted armchair. His head was down. His arms hung slackly by his sides. In one hand was a craft knife. In the other was a pebble-shaped piece of wood he'd been carving. It was still crude, but Callum could see a sleeping squirrel in it. Dad was making another carving, to replace the one Squirrel had thought was a nut.

Dad raised his head, blinked in the light. 'Where have you been?' he asked. His voice was steady. But Callum saw his hands were trembling.

Callum closed his mouth. He felt foolish, standing there with it open. And anyway, he didn't feel like yelling the house down any more.

Dad was a sad sight. He looked helpless, as if he needed looking after. Callum's protective instincts were stronger than his anger. He had a soft spot for creatures in trouble.

'I was in the plantation just now,' he said. 'I saw you with Nick. What's the matter? What's going on? And don't treat me like a kid. Don't just say that everything's all right,' begged Callum. 'Like you did before Nick moved in. Tell me what's *really* going on!'

Dad sighed, shook his head.

'Look at me!' said Callum, desperately.

Dad looked. 'I've taken something from Biogen,' he said. 'And I've given it to Nick. Who works for a rival company.'

'I saw you take it,' said Callum. 'I thought there was something funny going on.'

'What?' said Dad, startled.

'Tonight, when I came to meet you. I got past the security guard. I wanted to find you. I saw through a window . . . '

'Jesus,' said Dad, dragging his hand down over his face. 'What a mess! I must've been crazy! If Biogen find out, it means my job, even prison.'

'What did you take?'

'It's a bacterium—*Pyrobacter liquifaciens*.'

'So?' said Callum. 'You've taken some little bug. So what?' Then he remembered all the bio-hazard warnings on the incubator. 'It's not dangerous to people is it? Not some disease or something?'

'No. And Nick says it's no use to him. That his research is way ahead of ours. Says he just wants to check how far behind we are.'

'Don't see what you're worried about then.'

Dad took a deep breath. 'Well, in the first place I don't trust Nick. And in the second place, it's not just some little bug, Cal. It's genetically engineered. Man-made. It didn't exist before.'

'What's so special about that?'

Dad sighed again, as if the effort of explaining was too much.

'Tell me,' said Callum. 'I want to know—I want to know what's going on this time.'

'Well,' said Dad, in a weary voice, 'in some countries they already run cars on alcohol. In Brazil, in the Philippines. It's cheaper, more efficient than oil. But it's difficult to mass produce. You have to ferment it from plants with a high sugar content like sugar cane, sugar beet. You turn the sugar into alcohol. But *Pyrobacter liquifaciens* can make alcohol from any plant, even from trees. It can turn any plant material to sugar then to alcohol—in one quick process. 'Course, it's a long way from being commercial. It's only been tested on a very small scale in laboratory conditions and—'

'Is this going to take long?' asked Callum restlessly.

'You wanted to know, didn't you?'

But Callum didn't really want to know about the unique properties of *Pyrobacter liquifaciens*. What he *really* wanted to know was why Dad had taken such crazy risks for Nick. So he asked him.

'But I don't understand it. Why are you giving stuff to Nick? Doing him a favour? You nearly got caught back there. When the security bloke came looking through the door!' Callum felt his voice getting louder, more resentful. All his grievances and fears came gushing out. He was powerless to stop them. 'He hates my guts, Dad. I told you that! What are you helping him for? What are you even talking to him for?'

'I didn't have much choice,' Dad answered.

He paused, as if he was turning things over in his mind. Perhaps he was thinking of lying. But he knew, as well as Callum did, that he was the world's worst liar.

'Nick was blackmailing me,' he said. 'He had some information. He threatened to go to the police with it, unless I took the bacterium.'

And in Callum's mind, a nasty little worm began to twitch . . .

'It was about me, wasn't it?' he burst out. 'That information—it was something bad about me?'

Dad nodded, reluctantly. 'He could get you into a lot of trouble, Cal.'

'What did you believe him for?' cried Callum. 'I told you and told you. He's always trying to get at me, making trouble between me and Mum. Blaming me for things I never did. Like spilling coffee on the Chinese rug. So what's he been saying about me now?'

'This isn't spilling coffee on rugs, Cal. This is really serious—police business. Last night, when that car drove up. You know, shone its headlights at the house. That was Nick. He told me you set fire to things. Says he's watched you do it. He knows you set fire to the house. He says it wasn't an accident.'

'That's a lie!' yelled Callum. 'He can't prove nothing! He just wants to get me locked up! And how can he start blaming me? When he already told the police he did it?'

'He says he did that deliberately. To keep the police out of it. To keep them out of it until *he* wants them involved. He says it's no problem. That he'll just invent another story. Tell them he lied to protect you. But that now he's thought it over—and thinks you should be put away for your own good. He could do it, Cal. He's good with words.'

Callum felt his frustration bursting inside him like pain. He knew Nick had cornered him again. He clenched his fists. 'I'll kill him, I'll kill him, that bastard!'

'Shut up,' ordered Dad, 'and listen. There are other things he can use against you. He says you're always lighting up matches. That he's seen you set fire to litter bins. He knows other people who've seen you too. Mrs Petronelli from up the street—you set fire to her dustbin, didn't you? And she saw you. There are witnesses, Cal. And he gave me this newspaper cutting.'

Dad dug in the pocket of his jeans, smoothed out a piece of paper, handed it to Callum.

'ARSON ATTACK ON PARKVIEW HIGH,' read Callum.

'That's your school, Cal. It says there was four thousand pounds worth of damage. And Nick says you were out that night. Till very late. And the next day, after he heard the news, he searched your pockets. And you had matches on you.'

'So what?' bawled Callum, driven almost mad by his feelings of helplessness and fear. He felt like a hunted animal. As usual Nick was too clever for him. His lies weren't 100 per cent lies. They were subtle traps—part lies, part truth. So when Callum tried to argue his way out of them, he just tightened the noose around his own neck.

'So what?' he demanded again. 'I always have matches on me. I'm never hardly without matches. What does that prove? And I was out that night till late. 'Cos I stay out late every night, don't I? 'Cos I don't like going home, not with Nick there. But I never set fire to the school. I like going to school!'

Dad didn't look convinced, as Callum had hoped. His face was even more deeply troubled. 'So what about the litter bins, Cal? And Mrs Petronelli's dustbin?'

'Well, I did do that,' shrugged Callum. 'But I was only messing about. I mean, they can't lock me up for that, can they? I mean, did he really say he'd go to the police? Unless you pinched this *pryro . . . pyro*—'

'*Pyrobacter liquifaciens*,' said Callum's dad. 'And yes, I just told you, he said he'd go to the police. And I think he's got a good case. I think they'd believe him.'

Callum thought so too. Nick was very convincing. He thought the police would believe anything Nick said.

'You don't believe him, do you?' Callum questioned his dad anxiously. 'You don't believe I did the school?'

Callum's dad didn't seem to hear the question. Instead of answering it, he said, 'Cal, I couldn't take the chance of them believing Nick. I couldn't see you locked away somewhere. You've had enough to put up with these past few months. And, whatever happened, I don't think it was your fault.'

Callum looked at his dad in astonishment. Everything had been his fault lately.

'So that's why I did it . . . ' finished Dad lamely. 'I couldn't see any other way.'

Suddenly Callum felt a great rush of affection for his dad. He told himself, Dad stood up for me. He's on my side. He took those risks for me, not Nick. And the thought made him grin with delight and relief. He just couldn't help himself.

'You were dead brave, Dad,' said Callum. 'It was dangerous, what you did. You were a hero back there.'

Dad gave a bitter laugh. 'That's not how I see myself,' he said. 'And that's not how anyone else'll see me, if I get found out.'

'Well, I think you are,' said Callum, defiantly.

But Callum's dad wasn't listening. He seemed lost in his own thoughts.

Then he said, 'Cal, why did you do it?'

'What?' said Cal in a warning voice. 'I told you, I never did that school! That's the honest truth!' And it was the honest truth—he hadn't set fire to his school. Though no one seemed to believe him.

'All right,' soothed Dad, 'just forget the school for a minute. But why this fascination with matches and setting fire to things? You never used to do things like that.'

Callum shrugged helplessly. He used to be quite talkative. But lately he had become much more wary. Words just seemed to snare you, get you deeper into trouble.

And, anyway, he didn't really know why he'd had a sudden compulsion to burn things. It had started about two months ago with the match test. Seeing how much pain he could stand without flinching. Then he had set light to other things. Made bigger and better blazes, Sometimes he would stand close to them just to feel the friendly warmth. Sometimes, when he felt like a waste of space at home, he would make a fire, gaze into its red roaring heart and think, I did that! Then he would run away.

'I'm no good with words. I can't explain,' he told Dad. 'And anyway, I've given it up. I don't do it no more. Look.' He turned his pockets inside out. All his pockets—except for the inside pocket of his jacket. Squirrel tumbled out of his nest in a shower of peanuts. 'Look, no matches!'

The squirrel shot up the inside of Callum's trousers, squeezed out of the neck of his sweater and sat on his favourite look-out spot—the top of Callum's head. Callum grinned.

But Dad rubbed his forehead, as if he had a bad headache.

'What a mess,' he said again.

Callum tried to cheer Dad up. 'You ought to have seen Squirrel,' he said. 'You would have been proud of him. He went for Nick. Just flew at him like a Rottweiler or something. A Dobermann or something! Well hard! He just clawed his face to bits! Didn't you, Squirrel?'

The squirrel's wild, glittering eyes darted round the room. He was looking for somewhere to jump to. Like a furry frog, he made a great springy leap for the curtain rail.

'Nick was bleeding,' said Callum. 'He didn't know what hit him!'

Dad didn't rejoice, as Callum wanted him to. He didn't shout, 'Attaboy, Squirrel!' He said, 'You're going to have to let the squirrel go, Cal. If he leaps for your face, with his claws out, he could damage your eyes. He could blind you.'

'He wouldn't do that. He wouldn't hurt me.'

'He wouldn't do it *deliberately*.' Dad seemed eager to forget the stolen bacterium and talk about squirrels instead. 'It's nothing personal. He's just doing what squirrels do. They leap from high point to high point.' Dad made wide sweeping movements with his hands. 'Like from tree to tree. And if the next high point just happens to be your head . . . You have to take him back to the plantation, Cal. He can look after himself now.' He stopped, waiting for Callum to protest.

But Callum, to his own surprise, heard himself mutter, 'Suppose so.'

He knew in his heart that Squirrel didn't need him any more. Needed a wider, freer world of sky and trees and wind. And somehow, now that Dad was on his side, Callum didn't seem to need Squirrel quite so much. He felt very sad about letting him go—yesterday it would have been unthinkable. But, today, he could live with it. And another thing. The squirrel sweater was beginning to smell like the bottom of a rabbit hutch.

Callum held up a peanut. 'Come here, you pest, you waste of space,' he said, fondly.

The squirrel, its arms and legs outspread, came gliding down from the curtain rail and landed, *splat*, on Callum's shoulder. It raced down his arm and snatched the nut. Ground it to crumbs in its yellow ratty teeth.

Callum said, 'Will he still know me? If I let him go, will he still come and feed out of my hand?'

'I don't know,' said Dad. 'He might.'

That night Callum slept well. He dreamed about Dad. In his dreams Dad was Judge Dredd, bristling with weaponry, dealing out rough justice to scumbags like Nick.

In the pocket of the squirrel sweater, Squirrel slept too. His tail, a grey silky puff of fur, was twitching. What he was dreaming of was anybody's guess.

In the next bedroom Dad didn't dream at all. That's because he didn't sleep at all. He spent all night tossing and turning in sweaty sheets with, 'What a mess, what a mess, what a mess', rattling through his brain like a runaway train.

8

As Callum's dad drank his coffee, something was happening over in the plantation. A pile of dead leaves was rustling.

A giant wood wasp crawled out from under the leaves. It was a lopsided crawl. When the red-haired logger flicked her away he'd crippled her. But she could still fly.

She dragged herself over pine needles. She was warming up fast. Soon she'd take off, find somewhere to lay her eggs.

Bits of plastic blocked her way. They were clear and jagged, as big to her as icebergs in the summer sun. She negotiated round them. But she crawled through the pink jelly. It had white circles of bacteria growing in it. Her long ovipositor, which Callum had thought was a sting, draggled in the jelly. It broke up the white circles.

She took off, a yellow and black blur in the air. She had a strange, low, rackety buzz.

She landed on the first pine tree she came to.

The ovipositor looked like thin, whippy wire. But it was really a hollow drill. Powerful enough to drill through bark, into the wood beneath.

The giant wood wasp raised herself up. Her legs looked like yellow stilts. Her body bent into a loop. The three sections of the ovipositor locked together to make a tough, rigid tube. She plunged the tube into the tree and began to drill downwards.

At a depth of five centimetres she stopped and laid her egg. But eggs weren't the only thing she was leaving behind. She was also leaving the deadly bacterium *Pyrobacter liquifaciens*.

Before she'd even finished laying, the bacteria began to attack the wood of the pine tree, destroying it, turning it into sugar, then from sugar into alcohol. And, as it destroyed, it multiplied.

The wood wasp flew away. But she hadn't finished laying eggs. She'd visit several pine trees that day, inject several eggs. And, along with them, several million bacteria.

Then, her job done, she'd curl up again under fallen leaves and die.

9

Callum scrambled out of bed. He was setting Squirrel free today. He'd meant to go out early, before he had time to change his mind. But it was eleven o'clock before he woke up. In the plantation, the giant wood wasp was already dead. But, before she died, she had visited seven trees and injected them with eggs and bacteria.

Callum went clattering downstairs, with Squirrel perched on his shoulder. He was surprised to find Dad in the living room—he'd forgotten it was Saturday. Dad was sitting in the armchair, where he'd been sitting since dawn. He was cradling his fourth mug of coffee. Smoking his fifth cigarette.

He looks a wreck, thought Callum. And he's started smoking again.

'I'm going to let Squirrel go,' Callum told Dad. 'Like you said.'

The squirrel hurled itself at a plant pot. Began scratching up the soil with its front paws. It dug up an almond. It had tucked nuts into secret places all over the house. Its favourite place was down the back of the sofa.

It squatted on its back legs, its tail fanned over its head like a palm leaf. It could balance perfectly now. It attacked the nut. Disassembled it in five seconds flat.

'Oh, right,' said Dad, vaguely. 'Good idea.'

But Callum could see that his thoughts were somewhere else.

'Want to say goodbye to him?' asked Callum.

Dad stretched out his hand to try and stroke Squirrel. But it whisked off up the curtains. It hung from the rail with one hand, like a trapeze artist. And chattered angrily at them.

'Come 'ere, pest,' grinned Callum.

Squirrel was a comedian—Callum would miss him when he was gone. Squirrel was also a one-rodent wrecking crew. He was wild and uncontrollable. But, it seemed to Callum, he could survive anything. Even his home crashing down, with dreadful suddenness, all around him. Even the loss of his mum.

'Come 'ere,' called Callum again.

But, naturally, Squirrel ignored him. He didn't come, like a pet dog, when he was called. He didn't fawn around you. Callum had to wait until Squirrel felt like sky-diving off the curtains on to his head.

'Ow,' protested Callum. 'I'm not a tree, you know. I got feelings!'

But he didn't mind Squirrel treating him as a tree. Squirrel was tough and fearless. He didn't need anyone—didn't seem to give a damn about anything. Callum admired that.

'Squirrel Boy,' Callum mocked himself gently. He didn't really wish that he were a squirrel. 'Course he didn't. But, in some deep part of his mind, he couldn't help thinking that it would make life a lot less painful, being like Squirrel. Not giving a damn about anything.

'I'm going then,' said Callum.

Dad raised his hand in a weary salute.

'Cheer up, Dad,' said Callum. He wanted to bring a smile back to Dad's haunted face. 'Everything's cool now, isn't it? We're here together, that's cool. And don't worry about taking that bacteria stuff from Biogen. Blame Nick. It's all Nick's fault.'

But Dad wasn't convinced.

'I'm off then,' said Callum. 'Off to let Squirrel go in the plantation. But if he doesn't want to, I'm bringing him straight back home again. Right?'

Callum opened the door. Turned back.

'What if the loggers get him?' he said.

'He has to take his chances, Cal, like the other squirrels. You can't protect him forever.'

Callum knew this was commonsense. But somehow, it wasn't what he wanted to hear.

It was almost twelve o'clock now. The hottest time of day. Among the pine trees it was stifling, airless. It smelt of warm peaty soil and warm resin. And alcohol.

In certain trees *Pyrobacter liquifaciens* had been very busy. Since dawn it had been eating the trees from the inside. And, as it ate, it grew. Every two minutes the bacteria doubled their numbers. And there were millions of them when they started.

These trees didn't look any different. They were Christmas trees, like the others. But inside they weren't trees any longer. The heart wood of each of them was being broken down, digested, and changed into something else. The first one the wood wasp had infected was the most changed. Its heart wood, in places, was like an alcohol-soaked sponge.

Callum was trudging more and more slowly. It wasn't the heat. He was just reluctant to let Squirrel go. He found himself in the clearing where Nick and Dad had met. He recognized it because of the firebeaters. They stood upright, in their wooden rack, as if they'd been parked there by witches.

This is far enough, thought Callum. He stopped by a tree that was on its own, right in the middle of the clearing.

'Go on then,' he said to Squirrel. 'Climb that tree.'

The squirrel clung to the squirrel sweater. Callum detached him, prising off one paw after another. He placed him carefully on the ground.

The squirrel huddled among pine needles. He was no bigger than a toadstool. He looked like a grey speck under those massive, looming pines.

'Go on then,' encouraged Callum.

The squirrel looked at him with diamond-bright black eyes. But he didn't move a muscle. He seemed paralysed.

'You don't want to go, do you?' said Callum. He crouched down to scoop Squirrel up. 'It's all too scary, isn't it, the great big world? Don't worry, you don't have to go. You can stay with me.'

He opened the pouch pocket so squirrel could jump inside.

Squirrel did jump. But not into the safety of the squirrel sweater. He leapt on to the tree trunk. He hung there for a moment, hugging the trunk. Then he was off, faster than your eye could follow. He scampered upwards, defying gravity. Then scuttled crab-like round the trunk. He was a natural acrobat. He looked at home in the trees—as if he'd lived there all his life.

Callum breathed a sigh of disappointment.

At the same time, he smelt an odd smell. It wasn't the squirrel sweater—he was used to that by now. This was different. And it reminded him of something.

Then he remembered. When he was little, before they moved house, he'd lived with Mum and Dad in Jubilee Street. There was an old toffee factory on their street corner. It was closed down now, had been closed for years. But every

Friday they used to have what was called a 'boiling', when they made the rum toffee. And the whole street would be filled with the smell of boiling sugar and booze. You could almost get drunk on that smell. It whisked through Callum's mind that what he was smelling now reminded him of boiling day in Jubilee Street. He wondered why he smelt it here, in the middle of a forest. But then he forgot it. He needed all his concentration to track squirrel in his mad helter-skelter dash to the tree top.

Squirrel was shifting faster than you could blink. Going higher, higher. The branches trembled. He was here, no there! Callum shaded his eyes against the sun's glare, scanned the very top of the tree. It made him dizzy, staring up at blue sky through green spiky branches. He could feel the earth turning under his feet.

Callum stepped back, right away from the tree, to get a better view. Had Squirrel jumped, one of those break-neck leaps into another tree? The pine he'd chosen was far away from the other trees. He'd kill himself. Be splattered on the ground.

Callum's anxious eyes searched and searched. He stepped back again. Something crunched under his shoe. He glanced down. And just had time to register broken plastic, blobs of pink jelly . . .

Then the tree ignited. *Whoosh*, it bloomed into an evil orange flower.

Callum's mouth flew open in a shocked 'O'. For a second he stood, totally bewildered. The matches were still in his pocket. But 'Did I do that?' flashed through his brain. As if he'd suddenly got the power to set fire to things by thought alone.

Then raging heat blasted him, roaring wind and blinding brilliant light. Callum flung himself down. Wrapped his arms around his head. While behind him a crackling fire-monster gobbled up the tree.

Callum staggered to his feet. 'Squirrel, Squirrel!'

He rushed, coughing, through smoke and rolling sparks. Yanked a firebeater out of the rack. He beat madly round the tree, crushed those little scampering flames trying to escape across the forest floor to burn other trees. He beat them all to death and stamped on them.

No time to stand back, enjoy the show. It was spectacular, a twisting tornado of flame. Just the kind of sight that should have thrilled him. But all he felt was confusion and panic.

Then, suddenly, just like a spent firework, the tree fizzled out. The flames shrank right back and died. Callum stopped his manic beating and stood, panting. He was standing on scorched grass. A storm of black ash swirled around him. It flecked his clothes and skin—made him cough again. And the tree itself was a write-off. From the base of the trunk to its top-most branch it was a black, contorted wreck.

The smoke had already thinned. Callum could see blue sky again. The birds had started singing. It was as if the fire had never been. Callum would hardly have believed it himself. Except that, among the other green living trees, there was a crumbling black skeleton. Callum wiped his hand over his face but only smeared himself with more soot.

Even Squirrel could not have escaped that blaze. Callum felt a great wrenching pain in his heart.

It was my fault, he thought. Why did I let him go?

He called out again, 'Squirrel.' Though he knew it was pointless. Even if Squirrel were alive he wouldn't come running when you called.

* * *

Back at the cottage, Callum's dad, staring through the window, saw the tree go up like a bomb. He didn't know it was a single tree. He just saw a whoosh of fire, like a flame-thrower, spray up into the sky. Saw the fierce white-hot inferno. Then nothing.

'Oh no,' he muttered to himself. 'What's he set fire to now?'

He did two things. First he ran to the mantelpiece, checked behind the teapot. The matches had gone. Then he ran for the door. He went haring across the field towards the plantation, smashing down purple foxgloves as he ran.

He met Callum coming out of the pine trees.

'What the hell have you been doing?'

'Squirrel died,' said Callum, dazed. 'I was just standing there, next to this tree. And it just burst into flames, all by itself. And Squirrel died.'

10

'Spontaneous combustion?' said Dad. 'You don't really expect me to believe that, do you? You must think I'm really stupid!'

Callum growled. 'Grrr!' It was a sign of his terrible frustration. He was desperate to get Dad to believe him.

'But, Dad, I told you, I don't do that any more.'

'So you said. Have you any idea how dangerous a forest fire is? And what did you use for it? Petrol? That was no ordinary fire—it went up like a bomb. No one but a complete moron would start a fire in a forest. You're very, very lucky it burnt itself out, didn't spread. You can't believe how lucky you are.'

'I told you, I didn't start it. I put it out—I stopped it spreading! I was standing there and it just started by itself. The tree went up like a rocket. Boom! And why would I start it when it killed Squirrel. Why would I do that?'

'Don't ask me, Cal. I've given up even trying to explain what you do.'

They were back at the cottage. Callum couldn't keep still. He was dodging about like a boxer.

'For God's sake sit down!' said Dad.

'But I didn't do it! Honest!'

'The matches are missing,' said Dad, wearily. 'If you don't do that kind of thing any more then why do you need matches, Cal?'

Callum snapped. He felt Dad was tangling him in a sticky web of words. Just like Nick did.

'I *don't* need matches!' he bellowed at Dad. 'That's what I keep telling you! I don't need 'em no more. I got matches, yes! They're right here in my pocket.' Callum slapped his hand against his pocket, made the matches rattle. 'But I just carry 'em about. I don't *need* them! I told you! But all you do is yell at me! You don't even listen! You don't give me a chance.'

Dad shook his head, baffled by this logic and by his crimson-faced son, stamping about in a rage. He sighed. 'All right. Calm down. I'm listening. Just tell me what happened.'

Callum stood still, abruptly. He'd just thought, Be careful. You'll wake up Squirrel! Glanced down at the pouch pocket. No silky tail. Then he remembered.

He took several deep breaths.

'Squirrel's dead,' he told his dad.

'I know. Now tell me what happened,' said Dad, gently.

Callum sat down. Tried to clear the red rage out of his brain. He thought, I should take off this squirrel sweater. It was too hot for sweaters. Later, he decided. I'll take it off later.

He forced himself to concentrate. Tried to remember what he'd been doing, just before the fire. And, as he was thinking, he talked.

'Well, I was walking about, trying to find a good place to let Squirrel go. But everywhere I came to I thought, No, this is no good. And I stopped in that place where you met Nick, that little clearing, and I thought, You'll have to let him go *sometime*. It was really hot—and there was this smell. It smelt like Jubilee Street on boiling day. It smelt like when they made the toffee. It smelt like when they made the rum toffee, actually, 'cos there was this funny smell of booze . . . '

Callum did not notice but Dad had moved forward, to the edge of his seat.

'And I said to Squirrel, "Climb that tree", and I stepped back so I could watch him and then, oh, I forgot this bit, I crunched something with my shoe. That dish, that dish of *pyro* stuff you gave to Nick, all broken up. And then *whoosh!* the tree went up. I was nowhere near it, it just went up and—'

'What did you say, what did you say just then?' Dad leapt forward, grabbed his arm.

'Gerrof!' said Callum. He thought that Dad was angry again. But Dad's voice wasn't angry. It was desperately urgent.

'Did you say Nick dropped the dish?'

'Well, he must have,' said Callum. 'Maybe when Squirrel went for him. He must've dropped it. Because I saw it all broken and does that mean he'll go the police about me now?'

'Show me!' said Dad, gripping Callum's arm so tight it hurt. 'Show me where the broken dish is.'

Dad hustled Callum out of the door. As he was locking it, a muffled sound, a sort of dull *whump!* came from the direction of the pine plantation. At first, he paid no attention. Then a sudden glare caught his eye.

He turned to look. Hot orange light flickered in the tree-tops, like firebirds beating fiery wings. Callum had seen it too.

'See,' said Callum, pointing excitedly. 'See, I told you. There's another tree going up. Like a rocket, look! And I'm nowhere near it, am I?' Callum spread his arms wide as if he had nothing to hide. 'I'm standing right here! So it can't be me—I told you it wasn't. It can't be my fault.'

The flames had gone. Dad stared at the funnel of black smoke. It spread into a cloud, then shrank back like a genie into a bottle. His face was white, appalled. 'My God,' he whispered, 'what have I done?'

As Callum and his dad hurried towards the plantation from the south, a car was sliding into it from the north. It was Nick's car. And he, like them, was coming in search of a dropped Petri dish.

11

They were almost at the plantation. A muffled bang turned both their heads. To their right, in a row of green pines, blazed another mini-inferno.

They were close enough to hear the vicious, spitting flames. Close enough to feel the heat and see the tree shrivel and twist in its own white-hot furnace.

'See,' began Callum. 'Look at that. I told you—'

But Dad wasn't looking at him. He was gazing into the tree-tops where sparks, like a crowd of fireflies, were scattering from the burning pine.

'It's spreading,' said Dad. 'My God, it's spreading. There could be people in there, Cal. Go and call the fire brigade.'

'But—'

On the far edge of the plantation, another tree blew up. A gust of wind caught a fireball, flung it across the sky. It plunged back into the trees like a comet.

'Go on! And when you get back stay out of the plantation! You hear me? Stay out! It's a death trap.'

In a stumbling run, Callum started back for the cottage. He punched in 999, gabbled into the phone, left it dangling off the hook. Then trampled back in sweaty panic through bracken and foxgloves. A black smoke-cloud crept up from the burning plantation. It throbbed livid red. Beneath it, patches of forest glowed like molten lava. It was a landscape straight from hell.

'Dad! Dad!' There were people on mountain bikes in carnival-bright Lycra gear. 'You seen my dad?' demanded Callum. 'He went in there.'

'A little bloke came running past, told us to get out fast.'

'Is he still in there?'

The cyclist shrugged. 'He didn't come out with us.'

Callum ducked past the bikes, ran on.

'Hey, come back.'

But Callum wasn't listening.

Where he plunged into the forest the trees were still untouched. He could hear a faint rumbling sound somewhere, like a distant stampede. Glimpsed smoke in the distance seeping through the trees. But he reached the clearing before the fire found him.

'Dad, Dad!'

He was surrounded by frondy green. Except for the coal-black corpse of one tree, the tree that had killed Squirrel. It was quiet and still and hot in the clearing—like the eye of a storm.

Then he heard it—a rushing sound getting nearer, like rolling surf. His head twitched round. He saw a single flying spark, a whole blizzard of them. Then, at the end of the track, a wooden gate exploded in a fiery cross. And suddenly the trees on either side caught fire and the track became a tunnel of scorching wind that blasted him in the face like a hair drier on hot. Made him stagger back.

Flames raced greedily towards him. He couldn't breathe, as if cling film were stuck over his nose and mouth. The fire was sucking oxygen out of the air, flinging hot grit into his eyes. The gravel path was heating up. He could feel it through the soles of his shoes.

And then he was coughing, wheezing in a world of fire. The firebeaters ignited, like heads of hair ablaze. He staggered this way, that—didn't know where to run. Flames reared up, shrank back, sucking in and out like heart valves. He saw escape routes, darted forwards—they filled up with fire. The trees around were waterfalls of flame. He was trapped in roaring, crackling chaos.

Callum fell, gasping and blinded, to his knees. Tried to crawl beneath the smoke.

A hand yanked at the hood of the squirrel sweater. Pulled him into another world that was slimy, slippery, and cold. A hand forced his head down, slapped something wet and clingy over his nose and mouth.

Callum grunted and struggled wildly. 'Geroff!'

'Keep down! Breathe through the handkerchief!'

It was Dad's voice. Callum stopped fighting. He opened his eyes in a painful squint. He was crouching in water, in a drainage ditch.

'Keep your head down!'

There was sudden searing heat and wind. Callum ducked down, clamped the handkerchief to his mouth. The ditch water glowed red and gold like neon lights as the fire flashed overhead.

Then nothing. The fire had passed them by.

A red-bellied newt slipped between his fingers.

'Euch! Woss that?'

He hauled himself out of the ditch on to crispy black grass. It crumbled to bits as he rolled on it.

He took a deep breath. Big mistake. There was still no fresh air. The smoky reek of the fire tore at his throat like barbed wire.

So he lay for a moment, breathing shallow, with his eyes closed. His soaked jeans clung to his legs and his trainers felt as heavy as wet sponges.

Somewhere, high above him, a skylark started singing.

'You all right, Cal?' said a voice.

Callum opened his eyes. Looking down at him were two faces. One was Dad. And the other was Nick.

Instantly, Callum sat up.

'What's he doing here?' he demanded.

Their faces were black with soot. Automatically, Callum wiped his own face with his sleeve and saw that it was black too. His hands were burned. They hurt—but there was nothing in his face to show it.

He stood up so Nick wasn't looking down at him. There were flecks of black in Nick's beard. His face was so sooty, you couldn't even see the scratches Squirrel had made. His eyes were red and watery and sore. But the expression in them was strange—bright and fanatical.

Around them the plantation was like a war zone. The trees were reduced to crumbling charcoal. Some had red veins of fire still smouldering in them. But most were growing cold. Ash drifted down like black snowflakes. Crusted their clothes and faces.

There were wailing fire engines in the distance. The sound of their frantic sirens held no thrill for Callum any more. They were too late anyway. The fire had burned itself out.

'How'd he get here?' demanded Callum. His voice was sour with all the old suspicions.

Nick glanced at him briefly, without interest. But he did answer.

'Came by car,' he said. He looked out over the graveyard of black skeleton trees. 'Had to abandon it—it's probably burnt out somewhere.'

He said it casually, as if it wasn't important. But the next thing he said was important—you could tell by the excitement in his voice.

'You've got to get me more samples,' he said to Callum's dad.

Dad looked done-in. He was swaying with weariness. His voice was no more than a croak.

'What?' He couldn't believe what he'd heard.

'You heard me. You have to get me some more. Remember the bargain—I get the bug, and you get him.' Nick jerked his head in Callum's direction. 'No bacterium and I go straight to the police. This little lot,' Nick swept his gaze over the burnt plantation, 'should interest them. Burning down schools, people's houses, starting forest fires. God knows how long it'll be before they let him out. A danger to the public he is.'

'I didn't—!' began Callum.

But Dad interrupted. 'I can't believe you're serious! After what's just happened here. You know this wasn't Callum. It was no ordinary forest fire. The bacterium escaped, from the dish you dropped. Got into the trees somehow. You get alcohol, combined with resin, on a hot day like this—and pine trees spontaneously combust. That bacterium's lethal. It's supposed to be environmentally friendly, make environmentally friendly fuel. That's a joke! Just look at the damage it's done here!'

'But it works!' said Nick. 'It works brilliantly. And incredibly fast. With safety precautions, in factory conditions, it's what everyone's looking for! The fuel of the future. It's incredible! It's in a different league to anything I've got.'

'And just what have you got, Nick? All that stuff about your research being way ahead. You're way behind, aren't you? Maybe you haven't even started.'

Nick shrugged. 'That doesn't matter now. What matters is that this bug has got fantastic potential—it's worth a fortune. And I need to get my hands on some more of it. Or else my next stop is the police . . . '

Somewhere, at the edges of the plantation, firemen were beginning to hose down the smoking wreckage. But here, in the centre, Callum felt that nothing else existed but his dad and Nick, who held his future in their hands. As they argued his eyes flicked to one, then the other, as if he was watching a duel.

He had matches in his pocket. His fingers clutched the box. In the past he might have got one out and lit it—to comfort himself. But not now. He had no stomach for fires just now.

Dad's voice was hoarse with the smoke. But Callum had never heard his easy-going father speak like this, with such urgency and passion. 'You're not just bloody irresponsible! You're crazy! The only thing to do with this bug is destroy it. It makes conifers explode. We don't know how it spreads. And we can't stop it. It could cause the biggest ecological disaster the world has ever known. It's not just the commercial forests, like this one. What if it reaches the natural pine forests? In Canada, or the *taiga* in Russia? They're six times as large as the Amazon rain forest. And it could wipe them out. Destroy whole ecosystems. Think about it, Nick. No pine forests in the world would be safe. And the fires would spread . . . '

Dad opened his hands in a mute appeal to Nick. Then he turned to Callum. 'I'm sorry, Cal. I'm really sorry. I don't know if he really will go to the police like he said. But even if he does, I can't do it. I can't get him any more of this stuff. We've been incredibly lucky this time—this is only a tiny plantation, on its own, with no other pine trees around. So it can't spread—I can't see how it can. It's been contained. Cooked in its own fire. But next time, if it escapes again, if it gets out into the environment, if it spreads—it's just unthinkable. I can't do it, Cal, not even for you.'

Callum opened his mouth. Those familiar feelings—rejection, rage, betrayal—were already burning in his throat. But the sight of Dad's face made him swallow his bitter accusations. Dad's face was painful to see. It was haggard with anguish and distress.

Callum trudged over, stood by his dad. He raised his head. 'My dad's right about that bug,' he said to Nick. 'And I don't want him to give it to you, either. So—do what you like. Go to the police. I don't care.'

Even as he spoke, he was amazed by the turn things had taken, by the words coming out of his own mouth. Dad was standing up to Nick. Just what Callum always wanted. But Dad was standing up to Nick at the expense of his own son. Definitely *not* what Callum wanted. Yet, amazingly, Callum didn't resent it. He felt closer, more united with his dad than he ever had.

You could almost see Nick's quick brain calculating as he eyed them both, standing together. Even his silver tongue struggled to find words.

He seemed about to threaten them again. Then changed his mind. Instead he backed off. 'You're a loser,' he said to Callum's dad. He sounded like a bully throwing insults in the playground. 'You'll always be a loser.'

He stumbled off, through a no-man's-land of ash and charcoal. Callum and Dad stood and watched him go.

Defying Nick had been a brave and reckless thing to do. It seemed right at the time. But now Callum was feeling scared. 'Do you think he will go to the police?' he asked Dad. ''Cos I'm really worried about that. Even though I said I didn't care.'

Dad sighed, coughed, wiped his red, bleary eyes. 'I don't know, Cal. I don't know what his next move's going to be. He'll be planning one, that's for sure. But I don't think going to the police is on his list. It'll complicate things too much. Right now, he's desperate to get his hands on *Pyrobacter liquifaciens*. Nothing else matters to him.'

'So how's he going to do that?'

'I wish I knew.'

They walked to the edge of the plantation. All around them dead trees hissed and smouldered and collapsed, suddenly, into heaps of embers.

The first fireman who caught sight of those two limping blackened figures cried out, 'Chief, there's two people out there!'

And everyone, cyclists and firemen, stared at them, amazed that anyone could emerge alive from that devastated forest.

12

On Sunday morning, Callum gazed out over a landscape that looked as if it was deep in soft grey snow. It was ash from yesterday's plantation fire. Even the purple foxgloves round their house were grey. The plantation was a wasteland of black stumps. There seemed to be no green anywhere.

Callum chomped his cornflakes. He didn't speak, even though Dad was only two metres away from him. Dad hadn't slept—there were purple stains, dark as blackcurrants, under his eyes. He was jittery with tension—every sound made him jump. Callum knew he was waiting for the phone to ring, for a knock on the door. Something, anything, that would tell them what Nick's next move would be.

Callum himself wouldn't have been surprised to see a police car swing into their drive.

'Can't you figure out what Nick will do next?' Callum begged his dad. 'You're as smart as him. You're a Doctor of Science like him!'

Dad said nothing. He just whittled away at a piece of wood. Clean wood shavings went curling on to a newspaper, spread on the floor. Callum thought Dad was carving something to calm his nerves. But he couldn't see a shape emerging from the block of wood that Dad was turning round and round in his hands.

Callum tried again to break the silence between them. 'What you making now? Is it a carving of Squirrel?' He secretly hoped that it was. He missed Squirrel. He still looked at the curtain rail, expecting him to be up there, ripping geranium petals to shreds. He still had the squirrel sweater on. He didn't know why. Except that it felt cosy, like an old friend.

Dad looked up. 'I'm making some pine chips,' he said.

'What?'

'Pine chips. I've been up all night, thinking. And I've decided how I'm going to stop Nick trying to get hold of the bug.'

'You going to thump him?' said Callum, eagerly. 'Break his legs?'

'For Heaven's sake!' said Dad, exasperated. 'Is thumping Nick your solution to everything?'

Callum shrugged.

'What I have to do,' said Dad, 'is alert people to how dangerous *Pyrobacter liquifaciens* is. Show them that it's far too deadly to be used, ever. I mean, that plantation fire is only a tiny example of what it's capable of. It was isolated there—it couldn't spread. But if it had spread, got out of control . . . ' Dad shrugged helplessly. The scenes of global disaster in his mind were too terrible to put into words.

'But how's that going to stop Nick?' said Callum. 'He already knows it's dangerous. And he doesn't care. He said so. He said it'd be OK with safety precautions or something.'

'I know,' said Dad patiently, 'but other people won't think that. And if other people know how deadly it is, then it's worthless to Nick, isn't it? He won't be able to sell it, or do any research on it. There'll be too much bad publicity. So there's no point in him trying to get hold of it, is there?'

'Oh, right,' said Callum, nodding.

Then the full implications of going public with *Pyrobacter liquifaciens* hit him.

'Wait a minute,' he protested. 'Wait a minute, Dad. How are you going to let people know without ending up in prison? 'Cos if you tell people, about the plantation fire, then they'll need proof. So you got to say how the bug got out of Biogen. You got to say you took it, haven't you? And then you've got to say why—that Nick was blackmailing you. And then you've got to say why he was. And then he'll tell the police about me. And they'll believe him 'cos he's real good at lying. And then I'll be put away too! And then—' Callum paused to grab a breath.

'I can't just do nothing,' interrupted Dad. 'You know that. This is serious, Cal. Really important.'

And what about me? Callum was going to protest. Aren't I important? And what if you end up in prison? Who'll be on my side then?

But he didn't say these things. Instead he told Dad, for the hundredth time, 'That Nick's a real bastard. He's really sneaky.'

He was scared. Scared that Dad was no match for Nick. And that Nick would somehow come out of this squeaky clean while he and Dad would take all the blame.

But he knew, all along, that Dad was right. He knew it just as clearly as he had done yesterday, when he defied Nick after the fire. Whatever the cost, what they had learned about *Pyrobacter liquifaciens* couldn't be kept secret.

'It's a mess isn't it, Dad?' said Callum. 'And you and me, we'll be in real trouble, won't we, once all this gets out?' But he said it in a resigned way, as if he'd already accepted what had to be done.

Then Dad surprised him.

'Not necessarily,' he said. He gave Callum a quick, reassuring grin. Then carried on, flaking pine chips off the block of wood.

'What are you going to do?'

'Better you don't know,' said Dad. 'But I might be able to blow the whistle on the bug. And keep us out of it. It's risky. But it might work.'

'What if it doesn't?'

'Then I'll have to come clean and confess. Because otherwise, there's nothing to link the bug with the fire. But if it comes to that, I'll keep you out of it, Cal. I'll find a way.'

'I don't want to be kept out of it,' said Cal. 'I want to be in it with you. Whatever happens.'

Dad said suddenly, out of the blue, 'I'm sorry I thought you started that forest fire.'

Callum gave an abrupt, embarrassed nod. 'That's OK.' Then he said, 'So when are you going to try this, this whatever you're planning?'

'Tomorrow,' said Dad, 'at Biogen. I can only do it at Biogen.'

'Tomorrow,' fretted Callum. 'What do we do until then?'

'We wait. Keep our heads down. Hope Nick doesn't make his move first. Don't answer the phone or the door.'

'I'll go mad, shut up in here all day,' said Callum, already jiggling around.

'I'll teach you to carve,' said Dad. 'Unless your hands hurt too much.'

'Nah,' said Callum, waving his hands around. 'That's nothing.'

'So what do you want to make?'

In his study at home Nick had been thinking. He'd already planned his next move. But it, too, would have to wait until Monday morning.

13

Callum hacked away at his carving of Squirrel. It was made out of cherry wood. And it was supposed to be Squirrel curled up, sleeping, with his tail brushing his nose.

Looks more like a dog turd, thought Callum critically. Carving needed patience. And he had no patience at all—not this Monday morning.

Restlessly, he got up, paced the room. Dad was at Biogen now, putting his plan into operation.

Wish he'd told me what it was, thought Callum.

He couldn't imagine what Dad was doing. All he could do was wish him luck. He squeezed his eyes tight shut. 'You can do it, Dad. I know you can,' he murmured, as if his good wishes could fly to Biogen, seek out Dad and flutter around him like birds of paradise.

At that moment, Dad could have done with some luck. He had never been sure that this would work and now he was having serious doubts. He was hanging around outside the pilot plant at Biogen. The pilot plant was set apart from the main laboratories. It was a small-scale factory with stainless steel vats, steel pipes, numerous dials and gauges for measuring things like temperature and pressure.

Inside the plant they were testing *Pyrobacter liquifaciens*, to see how it behaved in factory conditions. People in white coats with white gloves and masks were putting the bug into vats with wood chips and water. Stirring it around with big steel paddles, heating it up and recording how quickly it broke down woody fibres into alcohol.

Today's testing materials were ash chips and willow chips. Those were the ones the technicians knew about. What they didn't know about yet was the batch of pine tree chips that had been sneaked into the plant by Callum's dad. He had also, while he was in there, made one or two other changes.

And now he was waiting for something to happen.

'Come on, come on,' said Callum's dad, fretting outside the plant. 'Look at your list of experiments. What are you playing at in there?'

Twenty minutes passed and he was still lurking about. There were no windows in the plant so he couldn't see in. And he couldn't go in. There was a red light flashing over the door and a 'No Entry. Testing in Progress' sign.

Inside the windowless plant a technician consulted her clipboard. 'There's another wood to test,' she said to a colleague. 'This batch of coniferous wood.'

'Thought we were only doing two today.'

The first technician shrugged. 'Well, it's been added on the list. And the samples are here on the bench. Someone must have changed their minds.'

'Typical—no one thinks to tell us. Better set it up then.'

Nick had hired a car and was heading for Biogen. When the technicians discovered the extra experiment, he was only two miles away. He had slept badly. But his eyes were bright with purpose. He was obsessed with *Pyrobacter liquifaciens* and its potential. He'd thought about nothing else all night. Seeing it in action, in the forest fire, had only made him even more frantic to get hold of it.

It's dynamite, he was thinking. You could do research all your life and not get a break like this. Companies would kill to market it. And in factory conditions—with proper precautions—there'd be no danger. It'd be safe, 100 per cent safe.

And even if it wasn't quite 100 per cent, he thought, the risks were well worth taking.

He'd even toyed with a new name for it—*Pyrobacter sharpii*, after himself, Dr Nick Sharp.

Nick was dressed this morning in a smart grey suit. As he drove he was turning round in his mind how he was going to bluff his way into Biogen. The choice was between a visiting scientist or a sales rep. for microscopes. Once in, he planned to hide out somewhere until everyone left, then locate the bacterium and steal it. It would be tricky, very tricky. If he couldn't bluff his way in, if someone challenged him, if he couldn't get access to the bug, if he couldn't get out again—there were a thousand ways the plan could backfire. Nick frowned. What he needed, at this precise moment, was some good luck.

In the pilot plant the lethal combination of the bug and pine resin and heat was churning round in the vat . . .

At first, nobody saw the tiny trickle of smoke that drifted up from the vat. It set off the smoke alarms, activated the sprinkler system before anyone noticed it. An automatic alarm went off in the fire station in the nearest town. In the pilot plant a fireball shot from the vat to the ceiling.

And, instantly, Biogen was on full alert. In its laboratories, chockful of flammable chemicals, any fire, no matter how small, was a major incident. Klaxons started wailing all over the site.

The fire sprinklers easily doused the flames. Callum's dad had counted on this. He knew that, under test conditions, the fire would be safely contained. Nobody would get hurt. But there'd be witnesses, plenty of them, to the explosive effects of letting the bug loose on pine wood.

The smell of alcohol and resin made the air reek.

'It's the pine wood,' one technician shouted to another, as they ducked through the drenching water to evacuate the building. 'It happened when we used the pine wood.'

Callum's dad, unnoticed in the rush, saw them running. He stepped inside the plant. The fire was already out. The smoke alarms had stopped shrieking. The sprinkler system was flooding the floor. But the fire brigade would soon shut that down. The only other damage was the blackened vat.

'Thank God,' he breathed.

But all over the site sirens were howling. There was maximum confusion—flashing red lights, alarms, shouting people. Everyone, in whatever laboratory, dropped what they were doing and ran out of emergency exits to fixed assembly points.

They left all the doors unlocked. This was safety procedure—so the emergency services had easy access. The security guard had left his post. He was wheezing around, shepherding people out of the buildings.

Nick pulled in to let the fire engines wail past him. He could see Biogen clearly now. He watched the fire engines drive straight through the main gates, through the raised barrier. Saw white-coated people milling around in the car park. Saw the empty glass cubicle where the guard should have been.

'Well, well,' he thought. 'It's my lucky day.'

And he drove straight into Biogen, unchallenged by anyone, and parked his car in the car park.

Callum's dad didn't see Nick drive in. Didn't see him slip into the unlocked laboratories. He had other things on his mind. He had to find a phone. The security guard's blue uniform was bobbing about among the white coats of the scientists and technicians. So Callum's dad slipped into the abandoned guard post and, crouching down in a corner, so he couldn't be seen, with the phone on his knees, punched in the number of a newspaper office.

He asked for the environment correspondent. He spoke quickly, his voice muffled with his hand, in case the call was recorded or traced.

'The fire at Biogen,' he said. 'Ask them about an experimental bacterium called *Pyrobacter liquifaciens* that breaks down wood into fuel. They were testing it in the pilot plant when the fire broke out.'

He put the phone down.

It was an extra precaution. Just in case Biogen tried to hush up the cause of the fire.

Callum's dad walked out of the box. He was satisfied no one had seen him—everyone was still crowded round the main buildings.

He felt light-headed with relief. He couldn't believe there'd been no hitches. That everything had gone so smoothly.

And then he saw Nick driving out of the main gates.

14

Two hours later, Nick was in the kitchen at home. He had sneaked one Petri dish of *Pyrobacter liquifaciens* out of Biogen. And now he was trying to grow some more.

He'd already prepared the agar medium—several dishes of pink jelly were lined up on the kitchen worktop.

Next he lit the gas hob, took a fine wire loop and sterilized it in the flame.

He lifted the lid of the dish he'd stolen, very quickly, so he didn't contaminate the culture. He dabbed the loop on to the white rings of bacteria and then dabbed it again on to the clean, specially-prepared jelly.

Nick was trembling with excitement. He dropped the wire loop. It fell on to the seat of the kitchen chair and he had to sterilize it again. But, eventually, he'd put samples of *Pyrobacter liquifaciens* into all the Petri dishes. Now all he had to do was wait. And he would have his own home-grown bugs.

He left the dishes, with the lids taped on and the bacteria inside them already growing. He needed to fetch a microscope from work. Then, for the first time, he'd be able to examine this miracle bug under a powerful lens. See what made it so smart. See what made it tick.

15

'But you can't be sure he took it,' said Callum to his dad. 'Maybe he couldn't get in. Maybe someone stopped him.'

'It would've been easy,' said Dad. 'All the doors were unlocked, the building had been evacuated. There was nobody in there. It was a gift. He could've just walked straight into the labs.'

'I bet he got it,' said Callum, frowning. 'He's a—'

'Yes, I know, he's a cunning bastard. And I bet he got it too,' said Dad.

'He spoils everything,' muttered Callum.

'What?'

'Nothing.'

It was five-thirty before Dad could get back from work. He'd wanted to leave straight away, to follow Nick. But he daren't. They were counting heads after the fire—it would have caused panic if someone was missing.

At Biogen things had been going exactly as planned. Better in fact. There was already a major investigation under way. And the press had come sniffing round. *Pyrobacter liquifaciens* couldn't be hushed up—it would be public knowledge soon. Words like 'ecological disaster' were on people's lips.

And, already, the company bosses had made the decision that research on it must be stopped. Until further notice.

But all this would mean nothing if Nick had managed to smuggle out some of the bug in his pocket.

'Why are you still wearing that squirrel sweater?' asked Dad suddenly.

'What, this?' said Callum, as if he'd only just noticed it. He shrugged. 'I just like it, that's all.' He couldn't explain. It was like carrying round your own little nest. When life got bad he could put up the hood and hide inside it. It had his things in the pocket—the gnawed carving of Squirrel, the dog-turd one he'd tried to do. His matches—the ones he was never going to use again. It didn't smell of Squirrel any more. Not much, anyhow. But he never wanted to take it off.

'You'll have to change it sometime,' said Dad, as if he could read his mind. 'You don't sleep in it, do you?'

''Course I don't,' lied Callum.

He knew, perfectly well, that he'd have to take it off sometime. But not just yet.

'You should at least *wash* it.'

'No!' Callum backed away as if Dad was going to snatch the sweater off his back. When Callum was little he'd had a tatty old comfort blanket. He'd carried it everywhere with him. And every time Mum wanted to wash it, he'd screamed and fought. Made a massive fuss. And he'd watched, with an anxious, screwed-up face, as it went round and round in the washing machine. Watched it flapping on the washing line. He hadn't relaxed until Mum had unpegged it and given it back to him. He and that old blanket were inseparable. And he was beginning to feel that way about the squirrel sweater.

'Look,' he said to Dad, 'it's not important anyhow. I mean, who cares what I'm wearing? We're supposed to be thinking about Nick, right? And what to do about him?'

'I know,' sighed Dad. 'I just couldn't face it, that's all.' He took a swig of bitter coffee dregs, shuddered.

'So what are we going to do?' asked Callum. He took it for granted that they were a team. Before, he'd felt pushed out, unwanted. Not essential to anyone's happiness. But now he knew he was needed. Looking at Dad, sitting worn out and hopeless, made him even more sure.

'Come on, Dad,' said Callum. 'Cheer up. It's not the end of the world.'

Dad winced. Maybe he was thinking about *Pyrobacter liquifaciens* on the loose, gobbling the world's great natural pine forests. But he said, 'You're right, Cal. Sorry.'

'So what do we do now?'

'Phone your mother,' said Dad.

'What?'

'Phone your mum. Be casual. Right? As if it's a routine call. But find out what Nick's doing, how he's been behaving. Try and find out what's going on. But don't mention the bug, OK? And if she wants to talk to me, tell her . . . tell her I'm not here.'

Callum rang up. Dad listened in, biting his lip. But he didn't learn much. Callum's mum seemed to be doing all the talking. Callum rattled off, 'Yeah, yeah, yeah, yeah, yeah, yeah, yeah, yeah,' like a machine gun. Then said, 'OK, Mum, call you later,' and put the phone down.

'Well?' said Dad.

'Phew,' said Callum. 'I got GBH of the ear-holes.'

'What did she say?'

'Well, she didn't sound very happy. She said she's hardly seen Nick lately. I think she's going off him, Dad—I really think she is!'

'Never mind that now.'

'Well, she says he never comes home and when he does he's in a funny mood. Worked up about something. She says he's been bringing his work home with him. Doing stuff in the kitchen. Making . . . making cultures or something.'

Dad tensed in his chair. 'You sure that's what she said?'

'Yes, she said he's messing up her kitchen with loads of Petri dishes and he won't tell her what for and she's mad because he's supposed to be doing it up—he's supposed to be putting in pine kitchen units for her but they're still in bits on the floor and it's only half done and that they've got this brand new pine furniture and she said all sorts of stuff like that. Not important. She asked after you though. She said, "Give my love to Dad." Did you hear that, Dad? She said, "Give him my love"!'

Callum's hope, that his mum and dad would get back together, was never far from his mind. And he just couldn't pass up any opportunity to plug it.

But Dad wasn't listening. He was deep in thought. And what he was thinking made his face white with shock. Suddenly, with a violence that made Callum jump, he smacked himself on the forehead. 'You fool! You bloody fool!' he said.

'What?' protested Callum. 'What's the matter? What have I done now?'

'Not you. Me!' said Dad. 'I just realized. How could I be so stupid? There's pine everywhere. In furniture, floorboards, everywhere. And it's all got resin trapped inside it! Get your mother back on the phone. Tell her to get out of the house.'

He cursed his own one-track mind. He had imagined *Pyrobacter liquifaciens* on the rampage in pine forests—an ecological disaster. The thought of wood becoming infected *after* it was cut down hadn't entered his head.

Callum punched in the number. 'She's not answering.'

Dad took the phone himself. 'She's still not answering,' he said.

'Maybe she's in the garden or something.'

'Get in the car.'

Dad's car was an old wreck. When he pushed it above fifty, the steering wheel began to judder. He drove, as fast as he dared, towards the town.

Callum's mum was upstairs, working on her exercise bike. The phone had been ringing and ringing but she couldn't hear it. She had her personal stereo on, listening to opera. She pedalled away, singing along with the arias at the top of her voice.

Downstairs the kitchen was warm as a greenhouse. It had been sunny all day. Even now, the last of the sunshine was making hot pools all over the walls and floor. One of them was creeping up the leg of the pine kitchen chair.

Callum's mum had pedalled for five miles. She took her headphones off and went for a shower. Down in the kitchen, a tiny wisp of smoke was coming from the chair seat.

Two minutes later, Dad was banging furiously on the front door. Red paint, blistered by the last fire, came away on his knuckles as he hammered on it.

They waited, peering through smoky glass panels.

'Where's your key, Cal?' demanded Dad urgently.

'Haven't got it,' said Cal. 'Didn't bring it with me.'

'Let's try the back.'

'What about your key,' said Callum. 'You've still got your key, haven't you? It's your house.'

'Oh, yes,' said Callum's dad, as if he'd forgotten. He sorted out his front door key from a clinking key-ring full of them.

Callum followed him into the hall. He glanced uneasily at the evidence of fire. The ceiling still smoke-blackened. The walls scrubbed down, stripped of paper, waiting to be redecorated. Then turned his head quickly away. He didn't want to think about it. Didn't want to believe that, a few days ago, he had set fire to his own house. A different person must have done that. Instinctively, he hunched his shoulders, thrust his hands deep into the pouch pocket of the squirrel sweater. The matches rattled. He yanked his hands out as if the box had burned him.

Dad was checking the kitchen.

'See anything?' said Callum.

'There's the Petri dishes.' Dad pointed them out, ranged neatly along the window-sill.

'What are we going to do with them?' asked Callum.

But Dad's eyes had moved on. He was checking the new pine doors of the kitchen units. Some were already fitted, some lay on the floor. They were fresh, clean, honey-coloured wood. You could smell the resin.

But everything looked all right.

Maybe, Callum's dad was thinking, there's no contamination. Nick knew his job. And it was a simple technique, to transfer bacteria from one culture to another. Something he'd been doing for years.

He began to feel a bit foolish for stirring up so much panic. His eyes went back again to the Petri dishes. Maybe his nightmare visions of an out-of-control superbug were way over the top. Maybe he'd spooked himself too much. These last few months must have scrambled his brain . . .

Then he saw the smoke and knew that he'd been right all along.

Callum spotted it first. 'Dad, Dad, look, that chair's got smoke coming from it!'

'Mind out of the way.'

The back door was locked. They had no key.

'Get out of the way, Cal.'

Callum's dad picked up the chair by the legs. Held it up high so it didn't contaminate anything else.

'Open the front door.'

'What you going to do? Be careful, Dad. It's gonna explode!'

Dad ran outside. Dumped the chair on the tiny patch of front lawn.

It was smouldering, but not alight.

'Stand back,' said Dad. 'Give me your matches.'

'What you going to do?'

'Burn it,' said Dad. 'Kill the bug now. If we wait, it might spread. Can't take the chance.'

It flashed through Dad's mind, as it had a thousand times before, how little they knew about this bug's horrific predatory talents. Did it spread through air, through wood, through other organisms? No one knew.

'Can't take the chance,' repeated Callum's dad, urgently. 'Hurry up, Cal, don't mess me about, where's your matches?'

But Callum, incredibly, shrank back. 'I don't do fires any more!' he said, his face white, stubborn.

'I'm not asking you to do it—I'll do it!'

Callum, reluctantly, handed over the box.

'Stand back. Keep right away!'

Dad struck the match, threw it. The chair ignited in a white flash, as if it had been doused in petrol. Callum and Dad staggered back, protecting their faces.

'Fetch the others,' said Dad.

'What?'

'The other chairs. They might have been touching. The bug might have spread through them all.'

Callum's dad wasn't going to underestimate the bug again. That would be a big mistake—he was sure of that now.

'Right!' Callum raced away.

Mrs Petronelli, back from doing her shopping, stood still at the puzzling sight of a burning chair in her neighbour's front garden. She was even more puzzled when Callum staggered out with another chair and chucked it on to the flames.

It didn't flare up instantly, as the first one had done.

'Don't think it's infected yet,' said Callum's dad. 'Burn them all though, can't take the chance.'

He went back for the Petri dishes. Threw them into the orange heart of the fire. They cracked and twisted in the heat, the jelly sizzled. *Pyrobacter liquifaciens* perished in the flames.

'What else?' said Callum, panting. 'What about the table?'

'No, it's some kind of plastic, not wood.'

At the top of the stairs Mum appeared, towelling her hair.

'What the hell do you think you're doing? Have you gone mad? What are you doing, burning my new furniture?'

She rushed out in her dressing gown. There was quite an audience now of curious spectators. The chairs were crackling merrily. Sparks and smoke from the fire were whirling off, above the house, into the grey evening sky.

'Whoops,' muttered Callum out of the corner of his mouth. 'I think you've blown it, Dad. I don't think Mum's very pleased to see you.'

Lurking behind the on-lookers was a strange, hooded figure. It was Nick. He had seen the smoke as he turned into the street, parked his car and walked down to see what was going on. As soon as he saw Callum throwing pine chairs on to a bonfire he guessed what must have happened.

He put the hood of his coat up, took cover behind Mrs Petronelli, and watched.

He saw Callum's dad incinerate the bug.

Saw him grasp Callum's mum by the arm and speak quickly, urgently to her. He spoke for a long time and as she listened she calmed down. Her angry disbelief was replaced by shock. She had to sit down on the garden wall. Nick shrank back further into the shadows, cursing his bad luck. He wished he'd taken a Petri dish to work, as an insurance policy. But he hadn't thought about it.

The neighbours were disappointed. They knew all about the goings-on at number four. And they were expecting a major row—*Jealous Husband Takes Revenge By Wrecking Kitchen*. That sort of thing. But when the shouting stopped and everyone, amazingly, seemed to be listening to each other, they got bored and drifted off. And Nick, deep in his own furious calculations, found himself, just for a moment, without any cover.

Callum saw him. And he couldn't resist it. He knew that it was stupid but it felt really good. He lifted his right hand. Made his first two fingers into the barrel of a gun and his thumb and other two fingers into the trigger. He aimed his imaginary gun straight at Nick.

'Bang!' he mouthed. And grinned.

He couldn't see the expression on Nick's face. Just saw his eyes glitter for a moment, deep inside his hood. Saw him fade into the blackest shadows of the alley then disappear altogether. Minutes later, a car engine started up down the street. Then that too faded as the car drove away.

'Who was that you were staring at?' asked Dad, squinting with watery eyes through the smoke.

'Oh, nobody,' said Callum. 'Nobody important.'

He felt light as a bubble. Free, at last, of that crippling load of frustration that he'd been heaving around for ages.

The fire was dying down. The pink glow of it lit up their faces. Callum moved nearer, rubbed his hands.

'Hey, this is cosy,' he said to Mum and Dad. 'Just like bonfire night. Remember, when we used to have a bonfire and let off fireworks in the back yard? It's just like it.'

Dad raised his eyebrows. 'I can't remember burning the furniture.'

'Well no,' shrugged Callum. 'But it was good, though, wasn't it, on bonfire nights?'

'Here, have your matches back,' said Dad.

Callum took them. He smiled gratefully at his dad. He knew that returning the matches was a gesture of trust.

And then, without even thinking, he hurled them into the fire. They spluttered a little like a dud firework. Then the box dissolved into black ash and melted clean away.

'I don't need them,' explained Callum. 'I don't need to carry them around any more.'

16

'So what's the problem, then?' said Callum, desperately.

'What?'

Dad had not been listening. He was thinking about something else. Something that had been troubling him ever since this bug business began. How had *Pyrobacter liquifaciens* spread—from the broken Petri dish to the heart wood of the tree? From the first tree to others, not next to it, but dotted about all over the plantation?

Of course, the problem was not urgent now that the bug was out of circulation. Biogen had not destroyed it yet. But they had made sure it couldn't do any more damage. They had frozen it in liquid nitrogen at minus 196 degrees centigrade in the cryogenics lab. Then locked it in a secure cold room.

And, even if they'd wanted to, they couldn't resurrect it. The press were on the case. 'Firebug Causes Red Alert At Germ Factory' screamed one headline. The fuss would quickly die down. But the bad publicity meant that *Pyrobacter liquifaciens* would stay deep frozen for a long, long time.

It was the best that Callum's dad could do. Only, he just wished he could work out how it spread . . .

'So what's the problem?' persisted Callum.

'What problem?' said Dad, forced to pay attention.

'The problem about you and Mum getting back together? I mean, I can't see any problem. I just rang her up, right? And Nick's gone. Mum says he's disappeared, hasn't been to work or anything. Hasn't even left her a note. She says she doesn't want him back anyhow. Says she was really stupid to have liked him in the first place. Can you hear me, Dad? She says she was really stupid! She says she should've seen what a creep he was.'

'Did *she* say that? That he was a creep?'

'No,' Callum admitted. 'Not exactly. But I bet she thinks that, don't you, Dad?'

Callum's dad was silent.

'So what's the problem? I mean, are you going home now? Now that Nick's not there?'

'No,' said Dad. 'It's not as easy as that. It doesn't work like that. Too much has happened.'

Callum scowled with disappointment. 'I can't see no problem,' he muttered. 'She thinks he's a creep. She doesn't like him any more.' He felt helpless again, caught up in events he couldn't control. He hunched up inside the squirrel sweater. He had seriously thought of taking it off today. But now he thought he would keep it on, just for a while longer.

'Look,' said Dad. 'You said before that we never told you what was going on. That we just pretended everything was all right. Well, I won't pretend, OK? I'll tell you exactly what's going on. Except you probably won't want to hear. What's going on is—that right this minute I can't see me and Mum getting back together. It might happen. But right now I can't see it. So I can't make any promises. And that's the truth.'

'Can't you be friends then?' burst out Callum desperately. 'Talk nice to each other? That's not promising much.'

Dad looked surprised. He opened his mouth, changed his mind, closed it again. Then he said, cautiously, 'I think we could manage that. Yes.'

‘So are you going home?’ Callum just couldn’t help asking.

‘For Heaven’s sake, Cal, I said “No”, didn’t I? Haven’t you been listening?’

Callum stomped out. ‘Going for a walk,’ he muttered. All this truth-telling was getting hard to bear.

He turned round at the door, seeking for some hope. ‘Did you say, “It might happen”?’

But Dad had gone into the kitchen. ‘I’m going home then,’ Callum yelled after him. ‘Even if you aren’t. I’m going home tomorrow. Phone and tell Mum I’m coming.’

He did not dread going home any more. Not now Nick was out of the way.

It had rained since the fire in the plantation, five days ago. The grey ash had been washed away leaving a bleak landscape of scorched earth, black stumps. There was nothing alive in there. No birds were singing.

Callum plodded along by a hedge at the edge of the burnt plantation. There was wild honeysuckle tangled in the hedge. Even Callum, in his gloomy mood, caught a noseful of its honey scent.

Whump!

Something furry hit him in the chest.

‘Squirrel?’

He thought he must be going crazy.

Then Squirrel dived inside his sweater and raked him with its claws. There was no mistake. Callum was delirious with joy. ‘Squirrel! You’ve come back.’

In his heart he had never given up hope. He hadn’t even dared admit it to himself. But somewhere, buried very deep, he had kept a spark of hope alive. That’s why he hadn’t taken off the squirrel sweater. Just in case.

‘I knew you’d come back,’ Callum told Squirrel. He felt prickling underneath his eyelids. Realized it was tears.

'Don't be so soppy!' he told himself sternly. He sniffed, a great big juicy sniff.

Squirrel glanced up at him with bright, curious eyes. He was as wild as ever. He dashed into the pouch pocket. No peanuts. Dashed out again and leapt into the hedge.

'Hey,' said Callum alarmed.

But Squirrel skimmed the top of the hedge like a surfer, and when Callum got level, leapt on to his head and rode there, keeping a look-out. He chattered angrily as a crow swooped low.

'Treat me like a tree, why don't you?' grumbled Callum. But he didn't really care. He was so thrilled that Squirrel had come alive out of the fire.

'How did you do that?' he asked Squirrel.

Squirrel stayed on Callum's head until they reached the cottage. Callum wouldn't have been at all surprised if he'd raced off somewhere. But he didn't.

'Dad, Dad,' yelled Callum as soon as he got into the door. 'Dad, Dad!'

Dad was in the kitchen washing his socks in the sink. He turned round.

'Amazing!'

'It's Squirrel,' said Callum, nodding, just in case there was any doubt.

'I can see that. Where'd he come from?'

'I was walking. And he just jumped on me. He knew me! Where've you been,' said Callum stroking Squirrel's silky tail. 'Where've you been all this time?'

But Squirrel wasn't saying. He was too busy wrecking the house plants, digging them up and cramming the tender roots into his mouth. He looked like a different squirrel now—wiry, almost stringy. And he was battle scarred. One ear was singed. And the very tip of his tail was scorched.

'Look, the fire must have caught him,' said Callum.

'Didn't get him though,' said Dad. 'He's tough, he is. I told you. Rodents could rule the world.'

'I don't think I'll go home to Mum tomorrow,' decided Callum. 'Think I'll stay here a bit longer.' He couldn't imagine introducing Mum to Squirrel. Plus Squirrel would do more damage than *Pyrobacter liquifaciens* to Mum's new pine kitchen.

'But I just phoned Mum,' said Dad. 'Told her I'd bring you home tomorrow. And she was pleased. I mean, pleased that you were coming home. And she said why don't we all go out to Sunday lunch, to a pub or something.'

'Did she?' said Callum. 'So are we going to?'

Dad nodded. 'Might as well.'

Callum felt torn now. He didn't want to leave Squirrel. But he didn't want to pass up the chance of having Sunday lunch with all of them round the same table, like they used to.

Then Squirrel made up his mind for him. He sprang, without a backward glance, for the door. And bounded, in graceful loops, across the lawn.

'He's going!' cried Callum, running for the door.

When he got there, Squirrel had disappeared.

Callum's face collapsed into disappointment. 'He's gone!'

'So what?' said Dad. Callum turned on him bitterly. But Dad said quickly, 'What I mean is, it doesn't matter. Because he's just outside. Living in the hedges and trees round the house, where you just found him. Go out of the door, go on. Take some peanuts.'

Callum went outside. Strode about, his whole body tense with hope.

'Aaargh!' Squirrel pounced, one of his flying leaps, out of a young ash sapling. Snatched the nut and scurried up the tree to eat it.

'See,' said Dad. 'This is his territory now.'

'I'll probably go to Mum's then,' decided Callum. 'But I'm coming back at the weekend, to see if he's OK.'

''Course he will be,' said Dad. 'He's a survivor. And I'll feed him while you're gone.'

'Can we go to McDonald's tomorrow? You know, for lunch?' asked Callum.

'Don't know. It's up to your mum. But you'd better change your clothes. You can't turn up in that baggy old jumper, smelling like a squirrel. She'll think I haven't been looking after you. Might as well dump it in the bin. That's all it's fit for now.'

'No!' Callum hugged the squirrel sweater protectively. 'I'll be putting it on when I come back.'

'Only if I wash it first.'

'You can't do that,' protested Callum. 'Squirrel won't like it. It won't smell the same to him. It won't smell like home. Promise you won't wash it.'

Callum's dad raised his eyebrows. 'For Heaven's sake.'

'Promise?'

'I promise.'

'And *don't* throw it in the bin!'

Epilogue

A pretty little pink beetle had flown out of the plantation just before the fire. Its name was *Xyloborus varius*, commonly known as a bark beetle.

It liked to lay its eggs under the bark of sycamore trees. But, if there were no sycamores around, the bark beetle would use other trees—ash, or beech, or pine.

Before the fire, it had been crawling under the bark of a pine tree. The first pine tree that the giant wood wasp infected with *Pyrobacter liquifaciens*. When the bark beetle flew away it was contaminated with deadly bacteria. Under its wing cases, in the joints of its pink legs, on its ovipositor.

It visited a sycamore first and laid its eggs. The sycamore was infected but didn't burst into flames because it had no resin. So *Pyrobacter liquifaciens* wasn't consumed by fire but stayed in the wood of the tree, turning it to alcohol and multiplying.

There was a busy population of insects in that sycamore. Burrowing into it, chewing the wood, laying their eggs. Eventually the alcohol would kill them all and pickle their eggs. Then it would kill the tree. But before it did, a few insects escaped, a few eggs hatched out. Insects flew away or wriggled to the ground. And some of them, like the bark beetle, carried the infection.

The bark beetle flew on. It whirred through the air like a spark of pink fire. It was looking for somewhere to lay its second batch of eggs. There were no sycamores in this neighbourhood. So it landed on a pine tree at the bottom of someone's garden.

Raider
0 19 271644 1

When Flora and Maddy start to research the history of the *Arctic Raider* as part of their school project on the local fishing industry, they stumble upon a mystery. Why did a member of the crew die on his first trip? Who was the mysterious captain, The Iceman? Just what did happen on that cold Christmas Day aboard the *Raider*?

African Dreams
0 19 271684 0

Leon, pursued by bullies, and Sarah, at loggerheads with her mother, take refuge in dreams about going to Africa and escaping from the constrictions and dangers of their lives in the north-east of England.

This is a realistic and sympathetic novel about the dreams and disappointments of two young people from totally different back-grounds, but who come together to find temporary relief from their problems.

Deadline for Danny's Beach
0 19 271696 4

When the fox Martha has been feeding down by the chemical plant dies of chemical poisoning, Martha realizes that the whole coastline is being poisoned by waste from the plant. What can she do to stop it? What about Danny, brain damaged at birth, whose only pleasure is collecting things he finds on the beach, when some of the things he picks up could be dangerous?

Can Martha's friends help her fight to stop the pollution? And can she really trust them?